WILLIAM WALKER

THE
UNLIKELY AGENT
A PAM WILSON MYSTERY NOVEL

Outskirts Press, Inc.
Denver, Colorado

The Unlikely Agent
A Pam Wilson Mystery Novel
All Rights Reserved
Copyright © 2007 William Walker
V2.0

Outskirts Press
http://www.outskirtspress.com

ISBN-10: 1-4327-0278-5
ISBN-13: 978-1-4327-0278-6

Library of Congress Control Number: 2006940388

Printed in the United States of America

For Jan,

without her there would
be no Unlikely Agent

CHAPTER 1
NIGHTMARES

Traffic on highway ninety-five was unusually light for Saturday morning as Pam Wilson drove from her house in Dale City, Virginia to her parents' home in Mt. Vernon. She planned to arrive by eleven thirty for lunch in Old Town with her mother, Betty Anders, followed by an afternoon of shopping at the Springfield Mall. They seldom got together like this anymore.

May in Washington can be beautiful, she mused, and this should be a great day. Pam smiled. "God, I am so happy."

She turned onto her parent's street without noticing. This area of Mt. Vernon had not changed since Pam was a teenager in the eighties. Cracked sidewalks, billiard table lawns, mature trees, and well-kept houses.

She parked in the driveway and bounded to the front door. That it was unlocked didn't surprise her. Inside the lights were on, that was a surprise, not at all like her frugal father.

"Mom, oh Mom. It's me. You about . . ."

Pam stopped in mid-sentence. What she saw did not

register in her conscious mind. Lying on his back on the living room floor was her father. A small black hole in his forehead, a halo of dried blood surrounding his head. Bill Anders' eyes stared at the ceiling but saw nothing. She fell to her knees and grabbed his lifeless hand. A wave of fear engulfed her. What if they were still in the house. Her gaze avoided her father but swept the room. For the first time she saw the devastation. Furniture overturned, drawers pulled out, the contents dumped on the floor, and the empty drawers tossed aside. Then a second wave of fear struck as she struggled to her feet.

"Mother!"

With blurred vision, Pam raced into her parents' bedroom. More carnage. Even the mattress pulled from the bed. Blood pounded in her temples.

"Mother!"

Pam's voice echoed in the stillness of the house. Her mother's sewing room had been trashed. Her father's office was strewn with papers, files, and empty drawers. The silent odor of death permeated the air.

"Mother!"

In the kitchen Pam found Betty Anders sprawled across an overturned chair. Clad in a white tee and white panties, one leg twisted under her, the other jutting at right angles to her body, her hair plastered against the back of her head. Globs of blood and tissue covered the floor, walls, and cabinets.

"No! No!" Pam screamed, and screamed, and screamed, until the kitchen floor slammed against her forehead.

***

Fourteen months later, Rick Wilson dressed for work. He was definitely a baritone, of sorts. "I can't get no sat-is-fac-tion," his voice broke on the last note of the title line from the Rolling Stones classic. "Thank God, I'm a better lawyer than a singer." Rick looked at himself in the bathroom mirror. He was a slender six feet, with wavy black hair and intense brown eyes. Some men project racy sports cars, exotic cologne, and polo ponies. Rick Wilson's aura spoke of cardigan sweaters, jazz trios, and Chinese takeouts. He finished knotting his necktie when he heard a female scream from the kitchen.

"That rotten miserable son-of-a-bitch!"

Rick was stunned as he rarely heard his wife talk like that, and certainly not in that tone of voice. She screamed again as he hurried down the hall.

Pam Wilson sat at the kitchen table, tears streaming down her flushed cheeks.

The Wilson's kitchen was prototype middle class with its white appliances, vinyl tile floor, and complimentary Formica counters. The post breakfast aroma of fresh brewed coffee and bacon lingered in the air. A child's artwork and mementos of minor successes covered the refrigerator. Only through the European village prints, decanters in Picasso style designs, and a small figurine of Munch's *The Scream* was the eclectic personality of Pam Wilson revealed.

Rick looked at his wife, early thirties, five-six, slender, light brown hair, hazel eyes, and a near-perfect mouth. He always thought she looked like a young Lauren Bacall. "Honey, what in the world is wrong?"

"Read this shit. That rotten bastard!" She held a folded section of *The Washington Review* and threw it at her husband. "Breaker. That damned Ned Breaker!"

"You mean his column, 'Exposé.'?"

"Yes!" Pam put her hands over her face and her head on the table. Slender shoulders shook from uncontrolled sobbing.

Rick looked at the paper. "What in hell. . . ." He read

aloud. "In May of last year, Colonel William Anders and his wife Betty were brutally murdered in their Mount Vernon home. Recently, a reliable source informed me that Colonel Anders had associated with known criminals, including one of the world's most wanted." Rick ran his fingers through his hair. He looked at his wife with a blank stare and read again. "While working for AID in Thailand he laundered money, and in Vietnam millions of dollars disappeared." He cleared his throat before continuing. "Drug Czars and Mafia Dons realize money shrinkage from theft is part of doing business. But at what point does petty greed become a death sentence? A neat little police report speculated the Anders were victims of crack-head robbers. Will we ever know who really pulled the trigger that Friday night?" Rick threw the paper on the floor, moved to his wife's side and helped Pam to her feet. They embraced for several minutes. Pam stopped crying but clung to Rick like a small, frightened child.

"What happened baby?" Rick asked.

"It was awful. I usually don't read 'Exposé', his stuff is so bad. But today, unfortunately, I did. Then that horrible morning came back again. It's like those nightmares I had after the murders. Oh Rick, this is terrible." They sat down at the table. "Do you have a few minutes, or do you need to go now?"

"I've got a few minutes."

"Can we make Breaker retract what he said? I mean, can we sue him for libel, defamation of character, or something like that? You can't just write lies like that about somebody can you? Maybe we can find out his source and make them tell us the truth?"

Rick thought several seconds before he spoke. "When you look at what he wrote, he really didn't say anything direct. Breaker is quoting a 'reliable source', and the local courts generally support reporters and such keeping their sources protected, unless someone is really damaged. He quotes somebody and then says, 'well what if.' It's like somebody says, Pam Wilson doesn't like animals. A dog gets run over in our neighborhood and I say, 'Could Pam Wilson have done that?' It's just an academic question, not an accusation. You can't sue somebody over that."

Pam snapped upright in her chair. "What about where he says Daddy hung out with known criminals, the money laundering, and missing money? That can't be okay."

"Stop and think. When I was with the Bartelle firm, I represented Tony Sarto in a personal injury suit; somebody slipped in his store and got hurt. We were at his place going over the case when his uncle, Angelo, showed up at lunch time. Tony had some sandwiches brought in and we all ate together. If it turned out that Angelo was a Mafioso, then Breaker could write that Rick Wilson associated with known criminals."

"Are you saying that what Breaker said could be true?" Pam's eyes blazed.

"No, of course not. He has enough of something to cover his ass. I'm just trying to show how easy it is to take things out of context." Rick looked at his watch. "I've got to get a move on. Are you going to be okay now?"

Pam smiled a weak smile and nodded. The look on Rick's face told her he doubted she would be all right any time soon.

***

Several days later Rick walked from the front of the house into the kitchen, went to the wall calendar, and pulled off a sheet, the date read July 13. Pam sat at the kitchen table, her face drawn and hands cupping a half empty mug of coffee. She had on the faded blue chenille bathrobe she wore when sick.

Rick poured a cup of coffee and sat across from his wife. "You feeling better now?"

"I guess so. Did Ricky get off to school?"

"Yeah. He heard you again last night. Must have scared the living crap out of him from the way he talked. He's afraid you'll die like his grandparents did. I explained you just had a bad dream like he does sometimes. He's not buying that anymore. He knows something's wrong and it upsets him big time." Rick paused and sipped his coffee. "Ricky wet the bed again last night."

"Oh shit, not again, and it's my fault. What is wrong with me? These dreams are just like right after the murders. I keep reliving every second of that Saturday morning when I found them dead and the house trashed."

Tears ran down Pam's cheeks. Rick handed her a paper napkin.

"When I saw Mom, I lost it and fainted. Don't remember anything until you got there. I must have come around long enough to call nine-one-one, but I don't remember doing it."

Pam was no longer crying, but the look on her face frightened Rick. "What do you think about getting professional help again?"

"I don't know. I found out later from a police officer the first shot didn't kill Mom. She was lying there alive when they shot her twice more in the back of the head. Maybe she cried or begged them not to hurt her. What did Breaker say? There was a 'neat little police report'?"

"Something like that, but you didn't answer my question."

"Last time these dreams went on for several months. The only good I got from the 'help' was one of them telling me that when I fainted, I landed on my forehead and probably got a concussion. That's what may have caused the nightmares. This time it's simple, that Breaker article triggered them again."

"I hear what you're saying, but I don't see how that article could cause these dreams again."

"I honestly don't know either. I got to where I could accept that Mom and Dad were victims of random violence. Then Breaker writes that Daddy was in the mafia and they were deliberately murdered. The nightmares started again the night after I read his article. Maybe it's like those kids who used to drop LSD. Look at them wrong and they'd have a flashback. I'm sure the bad dreams will go away again. I just hope Ricky can hold out that long; I just hope I can hold out that long."

Pam sighed. "And I may as well tell you. We have to go to his school next week. They want to talk to us about Ricky. It seems he alternates between crying in class for no apparent reason and picking fights with the smaller kids."

"I thought he was doing so well in this summer program?"

"He was until his mother's wheels came off."

"Just let me know. I can always get time from work for Ricky."

"Don't you have to go to the office today? You're not just hanging around here because of me are you?"

"Not really. My first appointment's in Alexandria. I told the office I'd go over the files here and save the time of driving into downtown DC and right back out again. I still think you need help. But you're not going to get any are you?"

"No." Pam's mouth was set in a firm, thin line.

From experience Rick knew what that meant. "Have you thought of contacting Breaker and see what you can find out from him? This stuff came from somewhere."

"I've tried with no luck, but I will keep calling. Let's get up. We can't sit here all day."

"You're right. What do you have on for today?"

"Spouses' reception at the country club, but I think I'll probably skip it."

"I certainly wouldn't blame you if you did, but the O'Dell firm is paying for our membership and two of the senior partner's wives are active in the spouses' auxiliary. It would look better if you could at least make an appearance."

I really hate it when he does his subtle pushy little thing. No, you don't have to go Pam, just screw up my career. Thanks a lot Richard. Hell, he's probably right, I need to get out of the house. I've had five nightmares in seven days. I've got to have some diversion. Might even meet somebody interesting. We've been so busy moving in I really don't know anyone in the neighborhood.

"You okay?" Rick asked. " You're a million miles away."

"Oh yeah." Pam started. "I was just thinking how nice it will be to get out of the house and meet some other women. Let's get going. You've got files to look over, and if I'm going out in public, I'd rather look like something other than a zombie."

"You always bounce back don't you?"

"I try. I always try."

Rick kissed his wife.

Pam watched Rick as he left the kitchen. She wondered aloud, "What in hell could Daddy ever have done to cause Breaker to write those horrible, vicious lies?"

CHAPTER 2
VIETNAM· I

Headquarters
Military Advisory Command Vietnam (MACV)
Saigon, South Vietnam
6 March 1971

William James "Bill" Anders, Colonel, United States Army, walked down the main hall of Building One, MACV Headquarters. MACV consisted of twenty-five various shaped buildings located on the northern edge of Saigon,Vietnam. The smooth grass, symmetrical hedges and white-washed rocks stood in grotesque contrast to the barbed wire and machine guns protecting the compound. During the height of the war MACV provided office space for some ten thousand people, military and civilian. Today, two years into the withdrawal of American forces, only sixty-five hundred people worked in the complex.

Bill Anders thought as he walked, *No wonder we stay in great shape here, have to walk forever to get anywhere. The Pentagon has seventeen miles of halls, I wonder how many we have here?* He looked at his watch. *After eleven, better get my butt in gear, I've got lunch at twelve.*

Anders quickened his pace until he reached a door identified as,

J28 - Fiscal Analysis

(The J represented an element of the Joint Staff reporting ultimately to the Commander in Chief, MACV, the 2 meant intelligence operations, and the 8 indicated a department within intelligence.) An outer office contained a metal desk and chair, four metal side chairs, and two combination file cabinets. Opening from this office, two doors led to ten-by-ten foot offices. One door was labeled Col Anders, Chief - J28; the other read, LTC Vortmann, Dep Ch - J28.

Sergeant Dale Garrett looked up from a stack of paper. "Hello, Colonel, how did the meeting go?"

Bill Anders rolled his eyes. "Don't ask. We haven't had any input on Vietnamization in well over four months, but they still keep inviting us."

"Send Colonel Vortmann next time."

"I keep trying, but he's too quick for me. Always has another meeting he's committed to attend. Like today. Have you heard anything from him?"

"Yes sir. He called a little while ago. Said he's having lunch over in Building Seven and then going to the Cambodia Incursion briefing. He'll bring any handouts, and take notes. Everything's set up for lunch. They have a back table at the Asian House for you. Specialist Daley is your driver and he's also on stand-by this afternoon. Do you need anything else, sir?"

"No, that's it."

***

Daley pulled his sedan to the curb. "Don't get out Daley. The guards will handle the door. You have a place to eat?"

"Yes sir. The 422nd mess hall. It's close and has some parking. The chow's pretty good. What time do you need me back?"

"One. Just wait down here." Anders' door opened. He walked past several South Vietnamese guards, who saluted, and under a brass sign which read:

ASIAN HOUSE
Operated by the United States
Department of State

He took off his cap and placed it over number 86 in shelves lining the entrance wall. Eighty-six had been his football uniform number at Texas A&M University. As he walked upstairs to the restaurant, Anders recalled the story of the officer who had left his cap down here, had a few cocktails at lunch, and then couldn't find his cap. He went upstairs, had a few more drinks, and came down again at two-thirty. This time only one cap was left. The man chuckled and put it on. It didn't fit. Anders smiled to himself as he reached the top of the stairs.

At the restaurant entrance, Club Manager Johnny Winn met Colonel Anders. "You table at back all okie, like you want. You come this way please sir. You waiter today Bao. He do good job." Johnny Winn was Vietnamese.

Winn led Anders through a large orderly dining room filled with four and eight seat tables. The crisp white table clothes and fresh condiment racks reflected a corner of Vietnam far removed from jungles and death.

Anders ordered a glass of iced tea and looked at his watch. *Twelve ten, that ass hole better show up.*

Weaving between tables Johnny Winn led another

Army officer toward Bill Anders. The new man's uniform identified him as Major Barrow, Finance Corps. The newcomer was of average height, ruddy complexion and somewhat paunchy. He looked wind blown and dusty.

"Good afternoon, Colonel Anders."

Anders looked up without rising. "How are you Major?"

"Not too bad sir. Sorry I'm late. Thought I had the old man's sedan laid on but he took off to Ben Hao for lunch. I had to grab one of Central Finance's jeeps and drive myself into Saigon. Would you care for a cocktail, sir?"

Anders shook his head.

"Do you mind if I have one?"

Another head shake.

Phil Barrow's Manhattan disappeared in three swallows. His shaking hand caused the ice in his glass to clink. "I've never eaten here before. What's best?"

"Lunch is always a buffet. This is Tuesday, either prime rib or roast turkey. You ready?"

The men ate in silence. After lunch, Anders had a cup of black coffee and Barrow ordered another Manhattan. Anders made no effort to hide his disdain of the younger man, but now, for a few minutes, that was forgotten. They sat and talked as two comrades in arms. What they might feel toward each other had become secondary to a common cause. It surprised Anders how little Barrow knew of the Cambodia fighting. Barrow seemed amazed at the extent of his companion's knowledge concerning an operation he believed highly classified. That so few American ground forces were committed to the campaign seemed to surprise him.

Anders glanced at his watch. "You have the information?"

"Yes sir."

"Who all knows this?"

"Just you and me."

"Good."

Barrow nodded. "Thank you, sir. The price still okay?"

"Sure. Half now, half when it's over."

"I was wondering if we could have more up-front money?"

"No."

Barrow shrugged his shoulders. "A deal's a deal I guess." He reached into his shirt pocket and removed a folded slip of green paper. He studied it for a few seconds before handing it to the Colonel. Anders slid it into his pocket and gave Barrow an envelope. "We both walk out of here and the die is cast isn't it? I mean, there's no way to turn back?"

Bill Anders stared at the younger man. "No, there isn't. When we walk out of here, you're committed."

For a second Phil Barrow looked as though he might get sick.

"Have a safe drive back to Long Bien, Major."

Anders and Barrow stood, shook hands, exchanged salutes, and headed toward the stairs leading from the restaurant. On the way out Barrow excused himself to the latrine. After Barrow left, Anders spoke aloud. "He can't wait to count twenty-five hundred dollars. What a jerk, what a pathetic jerk."

As Daley drove back to MACV, Anders opened the green paper. It read, 15 March.

***

"Wait for me, I shouldn't be too long." Inside Building One, Anders walked directly to the office of Major General Buddy Randall, Deputy Chief, MACV.

Randall's administrative assistant looked up. "He's waiting for you, sir."

Twenty minutes later, Anders slipped into the back seat of the sedan. Daley turned to face him. "Where to, Colonel?"

"The Republic of South Korea Military Headquarters."

Daley drove his sedan under a portico attached to a massive white villa. A South Korean soldier, in starched uniform and highly shined boots, opened the rear door. Anders emerged to clicked heels and a sharp salute. As he walked into the villa, guards on each side of the front door saluted with their rifles. Inside another South Korean greeted him and led him to the office of Lieutenant Colonel Jung Park.

Park saluted and then extended his hand. "Colonel Anders, how are you today, sir?"

Park, with a Masters Degree from Berkeley, spoke nearly perfect English.

"Just great. This time of year Saigon becomes almost livable." The men shook hands.

"That's all right. Monsoon season starts soon. Then we'll have something else to complain about. Have a seat please. May I get you something?" He emphasized something.

Park's oversized office included a conversation area consisting of facing sofas with easy chairs at both ends. Anders picked one of the sofas.

"No thank you. I just had lunch. I'll tell you what though. Do you have any tonic water? With ice?"

"Yes to both counts." Park laughed. "No gin, I presume."

"Not this time of day. Is he here yet?"

"They called just before you came in. Held up in traffic. Maybe fifteen minutes."

Park sat in an easy chair. A Korean soldier came in carrying a tray with a bottle of tonic water, a glass, and a small ice bucket. He poured the drink with studied skill and ease.

"We have some time. Before I let this date go, I would like to hear exactly what Khan has planned."

Park leaned his head back, pursed his lips, and studied the ceiling. "I should probably tell you nothing. We are buying information, and you're selling. Simple business deal. But without you there is no deal. So maybe you should have an idea of his plans. On Conversion Day, C-Day, as you call it, Khan will convert more than five million dollars of old MPC for new MPC." (Author's Note: Please see explanatory comments at the end of the chapter.)

Anders sipped his tonic water. "That's fine except for two things. Khan himself can't convert a dollar of MPC and if he walked in somewhere with five million dollars worth, he would end up in the local equivalent of Fort Leavenworth."

"Of course, you are correct on both counts. That is where I come in. We have identified several South Korean units where Khan's MPC can be mixed with ours for the conversion. Oh, after C-Day someone will notice. Your embassy will send a nasty note to our embassy, which everyone will ignore. Two months later all is forgotten. After Khan gets through, shall we say paying off everyone, he will have nearly five million left. Your next question: what will Khan do with the new MPC? As the Americans continue to leave Vietnam, you will not have another conversion. Khan believes, and I am certain that he's right, that by using the black market and the willingness of your government to prop up the South Vietnamese currency, within one year he will have converted his five million into over twenty million dollars of US currency. Good old US greenbacks."

"Damn, could he really do that?"

"My Masters was in International Finance, so I know a little about this. I would say his twenty million is probably conservative. Your next question, very logically, is where in hell did an Indian get five million MPC dollars?"

Even though Bill Anders smiled, Park was getting on his nerves.

The Korean continued, "About half from drugs and prostitution, the other half, I think, is counterfeit."

"It would appear you and Khan have this all planned out pretty well. Where does my information fit in?"

"As usual, you cut directly to the point. The logistics behind positioning that much money takes time. Once the money is in place the conversion must happen immediately. Even a one day delay could cause questions which have no answer." A footstep scuffed outside Park's office. "Ah, they are here."

The rear door to Park's office opened. A slender, bespectacled Chinese man walked in, looked around, acknowledged Park, and moved to one side of the door. Behind him, a tall, heavyset Indian entered the room. Park made no attempt to hide his excitement.

"Gentlemen, Rajah Khan, Bill Lee, this is Colonel William Anders." Khan approached Anders. As they shook hands, their eyes met. Bill Anders was orphaned at age seven and raised in poverty. His ticket to a successful life came with an athletic scholarship to Texas A&M. Rajah Khan was a street urchin in Calcutta at age seven. His success came through a ruthless disregard for the law and other human beings. Both were self-made, surviving through their own strength, although each in a different world. A spark of mutual understanding may have passed between the two men.

Khan and Lee took the sofa facing Anders. Park returned to his arm chair.

"Colonel Anders has the information you wanted."

Lee and Khan exchanged glances. "You understand our need for this?" asked Lee.

Anders nodded in agreement.

"It will take several days to move this much money into position. Then we must have the conversion most quickly."

"Colonel Park has explained all of this to me." Anders hesitated for a few seconds. "I would like Mr. Khan's personal assurance my twenty-five thousand will be in a Swiss bank account within three days after the conversion."

Lee spoke to Khan in French. Khan replied and smiled at Anders. "You have Mr. Khan's personal assurance. Do you have the date with you?"

Anders took a slip of green paper from his pocket and handed it to Park. Without opening it, Park gave it to Lee. Once more Lee and Khan exchanged a glance. Lee unfolded the paper and said, "thirteen March."

"I must remind you that this is the information I was given. I cannot guarantee its accuracy."

After another brief conversation with Khan in French, Lee looked at Anders and said, "Mr. Khan realizes we all float in the same boat. If one wins, all win. If one loses, all lose. We will proceed with what you have given us as the best information we have."

Khan leaned forward and stared directly at Park. He spoke to Park in slow clipped Korean. Park looked down at his boots and nodded his head. When he had finished, Khan spoke to Lee briefly in French.

"Mr. Khan regrets that we must leave so soon. Thank you both for your cooperation. We will not see you again Colonel Anders, and Mr. Khan wishes you well."

Bill Lee and Rajah Khan rose and left the room.

Anders stood up. "Can you get my vehicle?" He hesitated. "What did Khan say to you? From the look on your face it obviously wasn't going down too good."

"He speaks very poor Korean, but he got his point across. If I screw this up, he will kill me and my family. Slowly."

"A nice business partner to have."
"Colonel, this is very dirty business."

***

Late afternoon traffic slowed the trip back to MACV Headquarters to a crawl. Daley directed his attention to avoiding an accident. Bill Anders looked out his window at the swirl of Saigon. *It's done now. What did Barrow say, there's no way to turn back. He was right. On the morning of thirteen March, the Koreans will have Khan's money all ready for the conversion. Instead, our Army will swoop down on them and seize the illegal MPC. Five million dollars worth of it. I just wonder where this will end. Hell, people have killed for less than five million dollars. I wish I didn't have such a negative feeling about this.*

***

At another place in South Vietnam a telephone rang.
"Yes?"
"Barrow just got me the date, fifteen March."
"You want me to get Steve to pass it to the other guys?"
"Hell no Niles! I've told you I want him out of this altogether. Do you understand that?"
"Yeah sure. Who's going to pass the word?"
"You." A long pause. "Okay?"
"Yeah sure."
"Out."

***

Author's Note: Since the Second World War, the US Military has issued script to its members when they served overseas. This was their medium of exchange within the military community. Script, called Military Payment Certificates, or MPC, was used in Vietnam, issued in denominations of $10, $5, and $1, and each printed on different colored paper. In an extended operation such as Vietnam, MPC also became a medium of exchange on the local economy, with black market trading becoming rampant. To limit black marketing, to some extent, new series of MPC were introduced frequently. Each new series used different colors for the various denominations. On a given day, not announced until early that morning, the old MPC was collected and later the same day new MPC distributed on a one-for-one basis. This was a conversion, or C-day. By six o'clock that evening, the old MPC was worthless. Although never formally acknowledged, considerable old MPC was never converted into new MPC, creating a financial windfall for the US Government.

CHAPTER 3
GABBY

"**L**adies, let's all find a seat please." The speaker's badge identified her as the Spouses' Auxiliary President. "Our program's ready to start and until it's over we can't have the marvelous lunch the club has prepared. Let's all find a seat."

Pam Wilson stood alone in the lounge and restaurant area of the Springfield Country Club. Portable dividers and planters had been moved aside opening an area easily accommodating the sixty-plus women now milling around. The unbroken expanse of blue and gold carpet indicated this arrangement had been planned when the club was designed. While not one of the ultra exclusive clubs that dot the DC landscape, Springfield was resplendent with excellent furnishings and well coordinated accessories.

She held a punch glass and a partially eaten cookie. She had met the two partners' wives, who were charming, and an untold number of other women, none of whose names she could remember. The red border on her name tag marked her as a new member.

I hate this, one second everybody's talking then, wham,

you're alone. It's embarrassing. Starting at her neck, Pam's face turned red. *Oh dammit there I go again.* Pam saw half of a love seat empty and headed for it. "Anybody sitting here?"

The occupant, a woman about Pam's age, with jet black hair and a smooth olive complexion, looked up and smiled, "No, please sit down. I thought I might get stuck here all by myself. My name's Gabby Petersen." She was a red border person too.

"Hi, I'm Pam Wilson."

The auxiliary president opened the program, a welcome by the club manager followed by short presentations on the numerous activities available at the club. Emphasis was on providing quality services and recreation for the members and their children of all ages. As the program continued, Pam noticed Gabby frequently glancing at her. Gabby leaned over. "Do you live at ten seventy-nine Glen Leigh Street?"

"No, we live at ten eighty. Why?"

"That's right. You're on the other side of the street. We live at ten seventy-nine Green Ridge. Our back yards touch each other."

Pam turned red again as she faced Gabby. "You're the girl with the scarf on her head and the old jeans. I'm sorry I that didn't recognize you."

"That's okay. We've only been in for two weeks. I should have come over and said hello. Is your son's name Ricky?"

"Yes."

"He's in the same summer program as our boy. Adam's ten, how old's Ricky?"

"Ricky's ten too. He's going into the fifth grade this fall."

Someone rapped a spoon on a glass. "Ladies if we could please have your attention. The program is almost over."

The two women looked at each other and winked. Gabby leaned over and whispered, "Let's sit together at lunch." The auxiliary president glared.

I'm glad I came today. Thank you Rick for kicking me of the house this morning.

***

The program ended. The lunch, if not marvelous, was at least tasty and the after-lunch speeches short.

Pam and Gabby chatted. Pam was an Army brat, raised in the DC area. Gabby's mother was Spanish and her father a naval officer who left the service after four years and settled in Ohio. Both women graduated from college, Pam from Georgetown and Gabby from Ohio State. Pam worked several years in the Justice Department, Gabby with the FBI in Cleveland. They both liked the summer program for their sons, and knew they would love living in Springfield. Discussion finally drifted to their husbands.

"Rick's a lawyer. He was with the Bartelle Firm but is now with the O'Dell Firm. He's a senior staff attorney. Maybe he'll make partner in a year or so. We think it's a good sign they're paying our dues here."

"Probably so. Brad's an assistant division head with the FBI."

"Don't tell me you two had one of those thrilling office romances."

Gabby laughed. "Sort of, I guess. I worked for Brad in Cleveland so we couldn't date. We talked a lot and I had one of those crushes you get on your first boss. When he got transferred, we had a cake and ice cream party for him. Afterwards I was in the break room cleaning up when he walked in and said, 'Gabby, as of five-thirty you don't work for me anymore. Let's go out for dinner tonight.' It took us six weeks to get married. Come on, how about you two."

"I'll tell you, but you have to promise that under no circumstances will you ever tell Rick."

Gabby nodded agreement.

"Well, I'm a junior at Georgetown, it's Friday night, no date, so I'm in the library trying to study. This guy from the law school's there. He's nice looking, dresses neat, seems to hang out with people who laugh and joke around a lot, but you know, just no sparks. He's kind of been around lately, if you know what I mean?"

Gabby acknowledged she knew what Pam meant.

"He comes over and says a bunch of people are having an impromptu party, would I like to go? I tell him no thanks, need to study and all. He leaves. About fifteen minutes later one of the class hunks comes up and wants to know if I'd like to hit a party. I say sure. When we get there, it doesn't take him long to dump me for this blonde with huge boobs. I'm sitting on a couch feeling like dirt when this first guy comes up. He says, 'Hey great, you came after all, let's dance.' He ended up walking me back to the dorm. The next weekend he took me to a Hoyas basketball game. We've been together ever since."

"Oh, that's sweet."

"No, not really. Rick never remembered that he didn't tell me where the party was. I didn't go looking for him, I just happened to end up there."

Gabby laughed. "Your secret's safe with me. By the way, did you notice the tennis pro who talked to us?"

"You mean the tanned guy with curly blond hair, baby blue eyes, tight little butt, and great legs? No, I didn't notice him."

Pam and Gabby looked at each other, then laughed aloud. "Are you always like this, or did somebody spike your fruit punch this morning?"

"I try to be serious all the time, but usually I fail. Unless it's something that is really serious, then I get too serious. Does that make any sense?"

"I think so, sort of. The reason I asked was because he talked about his youth program, and with your lithe body I thought you must have played tennis. I played some at Ohio State and would dearly love to find a sport for Adam to get into."

"I agree with you. Ricky can almost hit a golf ball, but tennis would be great. If we suggest it, they will hate the idea, we need for them to think of it."

"That's for sure."

"Yes, I did play some," Pam said. "Mostly in Brussels when Daddy worked at NATO. I think they were afraid we kids would go out on the economy and get in trouble so the Officer's Club had all sorts of programs. Daddy retired in the late eighties and they stayed in the DC area."

Pam could feel the muscles in her throat start to tighten. "You may have heard about them." Pam's eyes began to water. She took a deep breath. "Bill and Betty Anders. They were both murdered last year over in Mount Vernon." Tears ran down Pam's cheeks as she covered her face with a napkin.

Gabby watched in silence until Pam's shoulders stopped their involuntary shaking.

"I'm sorry Gabby. I've got to go fix my makeup."

Before she could rise, Gabby put her hands on Pam's wrists. "No, I'm the one who's sorry as hell. I've heard of them, but I had no idea they were your folks. Look, this will never come up again. If you ever need me please know that all you have to do is call. I'll be there. You already have enough to carry around. Okay."

Pam smiled. "Thanks Gabby."

"Let's go do some face maintenance."

After they returned, Pam talked about the impact Breaker's article had on her, the nightmares, the negative impact on Ricky, and her fear of driving Rick away and destroying her marriage. She mentioned her unsuccessful attempts to reach Breaker on the telephone. Gabby listened sympathetically. Pam realized that since the murders Gabby was the first woman she had talked to about what happened.

"Good grief," Pam said, "I've babbled like a kid. We both have stuff we need to do."

"Stuff?"

"Yeah, you know, stuff."

"Oh, you mean girl stuff. I'll have to remember to use that on Brad."

As they left the club, Gabby said, "Hey, I've got a great idea. You talk to Rick, and I'll hit on Brad. Let's convince them we need a gate between our back yards so the boys won't have to walk around the block to play together."

"Sounds great. Let's do it."

They stopped at Pam's car.

"Are you going to keep trying to get hold of Breaker?" Gabby asked.

"Of course I am. I'm going to find out why he wrote that garbage about Daddy, or, . . . or die trying."

"Let me know how you make out with him."

"Don't worry I will."

CHAPTER 4
VIETNAM II

Headquarters
Military Advisory Command Vietnam (MACV)
Saigon, South Vietnam
25 March 1971

"General Randall can see you now, colonel. He said to please go on in."

"Thank you." Bill Anders opened the door to Buddy Randall's office and entered. The general's office was large. American and Vietnamese flags stood behind his desk. An oversized portrait of President Nixon hung between the flags. To his left stood a small conference table and chairs. Randall and a shirt-sleeved civilian sat at the table. Randall returned Anders' salute.

"Good afternoon Bill."

"Good afternoon General."

"Colonel Anders, Bill Anders, this is Jack Kirkwood." The men shook hands. Kirkwood was a slight man with thinning brown hair and a mouth that seemed too large for his face. "Jack's with State. He's out here looking into what happened to the South Koreans' money." Randall made no effort to hide a smile. "Why don't you tell Bill what you just told me?"

Kirkwood ignored the smile. "I'm here to gather facts, not to make judgments. The South Korean Government has sent a note to the Chairman of the Joint Chiefs, with copies to the President, and Secretaries of Defense and State. The Koreans allege that on March thirteenth, US military units attacked six of their locations and stole some five million dollars of MPC. We, the State Department, have been directed to draft a reply." He stopped talking and waited.

"Bill why don't you explain what happened." Randall motioned to a chair.

He sat next to the General. "Yes sir. Mr. Kirkwood, where do you want me to start?"

"Call me Jack, and start at the beginning I suppose."

Anders took a deep breath and began. "In the course of my job I have to stay in touch with all of our allies' senior finance officers. About two months ago I met with South Korea's senior finance man, Lieutenant Colonel Park. We talked about how long past due we are for an MPC conversion, and he mentioned that some people would pay good money to know that date in advance. When I asked him for more detail, he got cagey, but finally let it out that some civilian had a few million dollars of MPC he would want to convert when the time came. It was obvious, at least to me, that the money must be illegal."

Kirkwood had a lined pad and a pencil on the table in front of him. He had written nothing. "I understand what you're saying Bill and agree with your conclusion, but how does this get us to March thirteenth?"

"Let me continue. A few weeks later, I attended a meeting with our finance people at Long Bien."

Kirkwood had a puzzled look on his face. "What's Long Bien?"

"That's Headquarters for the US Army Forces. The main Finance Office is there, the one that coordinates all currency conversions. There I met Major Phil Barrow, who's in charge of the conversions. He casually mentioned that he wondered if anyone would pay to know in advance when a C-Day would happen?"

"Whoa." Kirkwood spread both hands on the table. "It sounds like you stumbled into a willing buyer and a willing seller. This money didn't belong to the Koreans at all?"

"That's right," Anders agreed. "The money belonged to a man named Rajah Khan. They planned using Korean military units to exchange his old MPC for new MPC. Since it's unlikely we will ever have another conversion Khan could, at his leisure, using the black markets, exchange what he had in MPC into US dollars. Park talked about maybe twenty million."

"Is that possible?"

"Park thought so, and I wouldn't disagree with him. Do you want the details?"

Kirkwood shook his head.

"Getting back to the story." Anders continued, "Khan had one major problem. The shear physical bulk of that much MPC. That and the fact he couldn't leave it anywhere for long without raising too many questions. He had to move his MPC into place the night before the conversion, turn it in that morning, get his new MPC after lunch and then take off. By the time anyone figured out what happened, he and his money were history."

Kirkwood began making notes. "Keep going."

"General Randall got General Graves' concurrence for me to set up a sting on Khan."

"That's General Graves, the Commander in Chief of US Forces in South Vietnam?" Kirkwood asked. "So this wasn't a back-alley operation." He made more notes.

"No sir." Anders wondered what a back-alley operation

looked like, but he knew this wasn't one. "I went to Park and told him I could get the date for the right price. He wanted to know how much. I told him twenty-five thousand cash. He said they would put it in a Swiss bank account for me. By now we knew sure as hell we must be dealing with drug money. Then I went to Major Barrow and asked what advance information on the date would cost. We negotiated five grand, half when he gave me the date, and half after the conversion."

"Let me get this straight in my mind. The actual conversion occurred on fifteen March. The Koreans, or rather Khan, lost his money on the thirteenth. I don't get the connection."

"I guess it does get somewhat muddled on the surface. Let me break it into smaller pieces. First, Barrow calls and said he has the date. We set up lunch in Saigon. He gives me a piece of paper with the conversion date, fifteen March, written on it. I get back with General Randall. He gets General Graves' final approval. So I go to a meeting with Park, Khan, and Khan's lieutenant, Bill Lee. I give them the date of thirteen March. They bit on it."

"Give me a second, it's coming together now, I need to get my notes in order. Colonel, you have more nerve than a broken tooth." The men laughed in unison.

Anders continued. "The rest of it played out like we thought it would. The night of twelve and thirteen March, Khan and his people moved more than fifty crates of MPC into place at six South Korean locations."

Kirkwood appeared incredulous. "That many?"

"Yes sir."

"I can see why he couldn't have that lying around for very long. Didn't the South Koreans notice the crates?"

"That time of night there aren't many people around. A few bucks and they look the other way. Let me go on. C-Day's usually announced at five thirty to five forty-five.

All gates close, and everyone has from six to eight in the morning to go to their Finance Office or an agent and turn in their old MPC. Then after lunch, one or so, the troops get new MPC. About two or three in the afternoon the gates open again."

Kirkwood stopped writing and thought for a few seconds. "This sounds a bit like a James Bond movie. Why fool with all the cloak and dagger stuff?"

"After a few years a lot of MPC gets into the black market. On C-Day when the gates close, the illegal money's on the outside, the good money on the inside. When the gates open at, say, three in the afternoon, the bad money's worthless."

"What about the GI's in the field?"

"As soon as they come back in, they go to their Finance Office and a special conversion's made for them. Actually, few men take any money with them into combat."

"Thank you colonel, please continue."

"At about five o'clock the morning of the thirteenth, the US Army swooped down on the Korean locations and seized the crates of MPC. Does that sum it up for you?" He was tired of talking.

Kirkwood finished his notes and leaned back in his chair. His oversized mouth relaxed into an almost smile. "Here's what's going to happen. I'm going to Saigon and brief the Ambassador, some of his people, and some of our State folks. I'll telex my draft response back to Washington tonight and get a hop home tomorrow."

Randall eyed the civilian carefully. "And what's in your reply?"

Kirkwood's mouth finally broke into a real smile. "Don't worry General. It's a piece of cake. I'll tell everyone back home that you guys did a bang-up job. I'll tell the Koreans that US Forces seized money belonging to a drug cartel. We regret if any South Korean personnel were inconvenienced. Short and simple; file and forget. Now, what's happened to the other players?"

Randall and Anders exchanged glances. "Why don't you go first, Colonel?"

"Yes sir. All I know about is Park. I waited all day on the thirteenth for him to call screaming bloody murder, but it never happened. On the fourteenth I called him, but no one answered. Finally I went to the South Korean compound. They told me he had been called back home on an emergency."

"Do you two think the South Korean Government was in on or at least aware of this?"

Anders and the General again exchange glances. Anders spoke. "No, we believe it was Park and a few of his people. His boss probably didn't even know about it."

Randall continued. "We have no idea where Khan went. Of course we never knew he existed until Bill ran up on him. Best guess is he's holed up in Bangkok. They let Barrow resign his commission and get out of the Army."

"That's all?"

"He paid the twenty-five hundred back. Jack, anything else you need from us?"

"Just one thing. There's a rumor that something improper did happen on the fifteenth in connection with the real conversion."

Randall expelled a deep breath. "Unfortunately it's not a rumor. After the conversion, Finance analyzed who converted what. They have a reasonably good idea how much money every unit should have to convert. They found four non-military outfits that converted about five hundred thousand each more than they ever should have had. The first one's CIA, the second is run by State, the third a part of the Agency for International Development, AID, and the fourth a spook outfit. We don't know yet who they belong to. Each of these has a station chief or equivalent running it."

Kirkwood cringed at the mention of State. "That's good, but what do you really have?"

"We're not sure. They're small operations, largely civilian, most of what they spend is official. For example, the AID outfit's in Nha Trang, supporting local contractors who work on roads and bridges. They lack the number of military personnel to account for the kind of money they converted. The bottom line is we have no premise to explain these differences, but it appears something dishonest went on. However, we will get the facts on this. Colonel Anders is heading up a team to determine what happened. Since none of these units work for General Graves, it will take a while to get answers."

"About how long?"

"Since we don't expect any of them to cooperate with us, I would say realistically two to three months. Jack, you understand that what I just told you is strictly off the record."

"Of course. That was personal curiosity, not an official question. Well, you have work to do and I've got to see the Ambassador. My driver outside?"

"Yes. Jack, if you need anything else while you're here please call Colonel Anders or me."

"I do need some more help of sorts. The Ambassador's with some French muckity-muck tonight so some of us are going to a place called The Asian House, any good?"

Anders replied. "Yes Jack, real good. Johnny Winn runs it. He's like a guy I knew in college who worked in a restaurant. On Saturday night when they had linen table cloths and napkins he was Jose' the maître d'. The rest of the week it was a hash house and he became Joe the head waiter." The other men laughed. "Also ask for Bao to be your waiter, he's the best they have, almost speaks

English." More laughter.

Kirkwood smiled openly. "If guys like you can keep your sense of humor here, I think we'll come out of this mess all right."

The men shook hands and Jack Kirkwood left. Randall walked back to his desk.

"Do you have a few minutes, I need to talk to you?"

"Yes sir, of course."

"General Graves told me to tell you personally how much he appreciates what you did. If there was any way in the world for him to recognize you and give you the medal you deserve he would do it. And he means that. But he knows it was covert. So you have an unending thank you from two General officers. That and a half dollar will buy a cup of coffee. But what I really wanted to see you about is I have good news and bad news for you."

"Let's have the good news. After that maybe the bad won't seem quite so bad."

"Colonel William Anders, you have been selected to attend the Industrial College of the Armed Forces, ICAF. Congratulations!"

Anders made no attempt to hide his pleasure. "Thank you, Sir. You can't imagine how much I have wanted this. Yes, this is very good news."

"Bill, you would have the War College if you had stayed in the Infantry."

Anders started to speak. "I realize Sir, but - -"

Randall held his hand, palm out, in front of his face. "Wait. I'm fully aware of why you did what you did. Remember I'm the one who approved your using bootstrap at Georgetown University to complete your law degree. I knew then the Infantry was losing you. Surely the Army has use for good attorneys too. I think." Randall laughed. His fondness for the junior office was obvious. "Anyway, that's not all of it. You're going to stay on assigned to the

ICAF staff and faculty. I believe it's the International Fiscal Policy Department. Again, congratulations."

"Thank you again, Sir. You said bad news?"

"Since you're going to staff and faculty, you have to report there early. I've got to get you out of here in less than three weeks."

"I have almost four months left on my tour."

"General Graves approved your early release today. Said you sure as hell deserve it."

"What about the study?"

"Due to the draw down of people, I can't replace you. Vortmann will take over as Chief of J28. That means he will also head the study. Do you think he can handle it? Don't you two guys go back a long way?"

"We went through college together and both played football. Our last year we roomed together. But in all honesty, we have never been that close. He got his law degree while on ROTC duty at Louisville University and made a branch transfer like I did. Personnel Operations sent him here, I didn't request him. Not that I mind for a second that he's here. He's certainly a first rate officer."

"But you're senior?"

"Yes Sir. Those three early promotions I got put me ahead of all my peers."

"Bill, we went through hell together at Phu Lan. I have to know your real feelings about Vortmann. This study means a great deal to the Chief and me. We believe some really bad shit went on, done by our own people, not some foreign nationals."

"Sir, Dutch has great intelligence and even greater ability. Back then his weakness was doing just enough to get by. He could have played first string at Texas A&M, but he wouldn't work that hard. He would rather chase girls and drink. Anyway, General, I don't bad mouth a fellow officer. I sincerely believe he can do it. I have almost three weeks to bring him up to speed."

"Fair enough, Bill. We both have work to do. I'll get with you before you ship out."

***

Anders sat in his office. He had to let his wife Betty know that in a few weeks she would move again. Indian Town Gap, Pennsylvania. The best approach would be to send a military telex to Personnel Operations in Washington requesting they contact his wife and advise her of their pending move. He could write her tonight with all the details. He drafted the telex in long hand and had Sergeant Garret take it to the communications office. Bill walked next door. Dutch wasn't there. He went back to his office and sat at his desk. Buddy Randall had mentioned Phu Lan. It was an event that linked him to Bill Anders in a manner only men who have experienced war can comprehend. During his first tour in Vietnam, Anders served as an advisor to the South Vietnamese Army, working for then Lieutenant Colonel Randall. Over their objections, Anders' unit sent out a patrol composed of fifty Vietnamese and three of Anders' men. They were ambushed by the VC. Only four South Vietnamese survived. Three very good men had died. Men who had reported to and trusted Bill Anders. His career as a combat officer was over.

As he would later say, "Let someone else send men to die. I've seen too much death in my life already."

Anders' mind returned to the present. He spoke aloud. "Damn I wish I could get this feeling of doom out of my mind. People like Khan don't lose that kind of money and just shrug it off."

An even worse thought kept coming to his mind, I'm

almost certain the extra MPC converted came from some type of illegal operation. Sending Dutch to look into what happened is exactly like having a fox guard the hen house.

CHAPTER 5
THE PLAN

FRIDAY morning 8:45 A.M. the telephone rang.

"Petersen residence."

"Gabby, it's Pam."

"Hi gal, how ya' doing?"

"Super. Can we catch lunch today?"

Pam's voice projected an obvious sense of urgency. After a brief hesitation Gabby replied, "I'm easy. When and where?"

***

Pam and Gabby followed the hostess. Pam gestured as she spoke. "Over there in the corner looks great."

The women studied the menu without speaking. Their waitress came to the table. "What's really good today?" Pam asked.

"Our special this Friday is Lobster Newburg on toast tips. The vegetable's asparagus with our special orange hollandaise sauce. We also have - -"

Pam interrupted, "That's fat free, right?"

They all laughed. "Of course."

Pam and Gabby looked at each other and nodded in unison.

Gabby looked first at the waitress then at Pam. "Two glasses of Chardonnay?"

"Chardonnay with lobster's understood."

"I'll have your wine in a second."

Gabby took the restaurant in with one sweeping glance. The brocade wall covering, expensive carpet, linen table cloths, and leather chairs blended together in perfect harmony. "Le Café, it's really a swanky place. Brad and I haven't eaten here yet but I've heard the food's great. Pam, can't we do this dutch?"

"No way. As great as you were at the club and now letting Ricky stay with you after school on the days that I work, it's the least I owe you."

Their conversation flowed at an airy pace; how much the boys liked school, Ricky's doing better, the neighborhood's great, and so much at the club for their husbands and sons.

Gabby asked, "Isn't that bookstore where you work somewhere around the restaurant?"

"Un huh. One block over."

"How'd you get into books?"

"I've known Lindsey Sims, the girl that owns it, for years. We went to college together. When Rick and I moved up to Springfield, Lindsey needed part-time help. It's only Tuesday and Thursday for about four to five hours, but I like the mad money and getting out with people."

"That's what I like about working for Mr. Klein," Gabby said, "he's the Klein of Klein and Abraham over in Alexandria. They're interior designers. I only work when he has a model house to do. He gives me full reign on what to do and how to do it. Couldn't ask for more than that."

"Weren't you with the FBI when you met Brad? That's

a long way from interior design."

"When Brad became an Assistance Division Manager he was so high up that he couldn't have a wife in the Bureau. I had to find a new line of work. I went to a design school over in Falls Church for a year. In fact they got me hooked up with Klein."

Their food arrived and Gabby started eating. Pam took a deep breath. *All she can do is laugh at me. No Gabby wouldn't laugh, but she can say no.*

"Gabby do you remember when I told you about my asking Ned Breaker where he got the information for his story?"

"Sure."

"Well after a lot of calls, I finally got him on the phone."

"And?"

"He's a first rate jerk. He said he didn't disclose any of his sources to anybody ever. He's rude and obnoxious. Told me to take a hike and leave him alone."

"Did you tell him you're the Anders' daughter?"

"Yeah. He told me anyone can make up stories about who they think they are. In short, he said I lied. Like I said, he's a first rate jerk." Pam's emotions were rising.

"So what's next. You're not giving up are you?"

"No way! You remember the woman who spoke at the club about plants? The one who works at *The Review*."

Gabby nodded.

"She said to call her if we had questions or needed help. I called and went to see her yesterday."

"Great, but what's that have to do with Ned Breaker?"

Pam picked at her lunch. "After we had discussed annuals for a while, I asked her about Breaker. And get this, she went right through the roof. She said he's a cheapskate, a womanizer, a lush, a liar and a . . . a . . . a . . . lounge lizard!"

"Lounge lizard?" Gabby fought laughter.

"Yes. But get this. Every Thursday after work some of the staff writers and columnists meet for dinner with the Managing Editor until about seven-thirty. Since *The Review* pays for it, Breaker always goes. Afterward he heads to the Convention Center Hotel where he hangs out at the bar leeching drinks and trying to pick up something for free." Pam's cheeks flushed.

"So?"

Pam ignored her food. Starting with another deep breath she spent the next ten minutes explaining her plan to Gabby, who listened with ever widening eyes. Then Pam was silent. She bit her lip and looked directly at Gabby. *Oh great, now I'll have lipstick all over my teeth.*

Gabby paused in thought. "Let me get you straight. Rick's going to be out of town next Thursday night? And you want to . . .?" Gabby's brows arched in a question.

With her mouth set in an unyielding line, Pam acknowledged her plan with a nod.

Gabby motioned to the waitress, pointed to her wine glass, and held two fingers in the air.

"What're you doing?" Pam asked, "We don't need another glass of wine at lunch."

"When the waitress gets here, have her heat up your lunch, it's super. Eat it 'cause you're going to need all your strength. If we only have one week to plan this, we've got to get on the ball. I do stuff like this better with another glass of wine."

***

"Rick what time does your flight leave?" Pam asked from the kitchen. It was Thursday, a week since she had lunch with Gabby.

"We're on a two-thirty out of National."

"Honey. It's the Ronald Reagan National now."

"It's been National all my life, it'll always be National. I'm leaving the car over there so you won't have to pick me up Friday. We ought to get back about seven. You want to go out for dinner?"

"Don't they feed you on the plane?"

"You call that food? Get a sitter and let's go to Le Café."

"Rick, that place costs an arm and a leg."

"Aren't you worth it?"

"Damn right I am!"

Rick smiled at his wife. "What's on your calendar today?"

"Work for Lindsey this afternoon. Gabby wants to go out tonight. Girl's night out."

"Have fun and stay out of trouble."

"Which one do you want me to do?"

CHAPTER 6
BREAKER

"**W**hat time is it?"

"Where's your watch?"

"I like a bracelet better with this outfit. What time is it, Gabby?"

Gabby smiled and shook her head. "It's two minutes later than the last time you asked me. Seven twenty four."

"What if he doesn't show up?"

"I did a little checking on my own. The information that woman from *The Review* gave you was right. They meet for an early dinner and break up about seven-thirty. Today they're going to the Italian restaurant around the corner. So give him five minutes or so to walk over. Don't worry he'll show."

"That suite we have costs over three hundred and fifty dollars a night. That's my mad money for a month."

"I know, but I couldn't get a Government discount through Brad. Guess the lounge lizard really better show up, huh?"

The Convention Center Hotel's lobby bar marked the crossroads of Washington, DC. Politicians, diplomats, industrialists and tourists drank here sharing space with local residents. It existed to impress with a forty-foot mahogany bar, brass and dark leather stools, and two dozen matching tables and chairs.

When viewed by a casual observer, two friends listened to canned music while they enjoyed a glass of wine and exchanged light conversation. One might note the slender brunette's rather short skirt and seductive low-cut top. Her friend's dark good looks were enhanced by a jade green "button up the front" dress. The several missed buttons were no doubt due to carelessness.

One of the bartenders was enjoying the scenery. *I feel sorry for the guy those babes latch onto. The poor slob won't have a chance. They're pros.*

"Okay Pam. We're probably only going to get one shot at Breaker. If we do or say something that comes across wrong he may very well cutout. We have a few minutes to kill, let's go over our stories again."

Pam cocked her head to one side, sat her wine glass on the table, and recited. "My name's JoAnne Gorman and I do rewrite for a Baltimore paper. I've had a few things under my own by-line. Have you seen any of them? What I need is one break to start making it big. I can't tell you how I know this, but there's some dirty business with the school board. I read your column all the time. How do you find the people who give you that inside information? What really caught my eye was that one you did about the Fourth of July and that Army guy. That's a fourteen-month old story. How did you do it? If I knew how to come onto the right people in the right way, I think I could break the school board thing wide open."

Pam continued with names, addresses, and events general enough to be meaningless, but sounding factual on the surface.

Gabby had a simpler script and cover. Her name was

Mary Ranson, JoAnne's best friend. She worked in real estate, and came along with JoAnne for a lark. Both women welcomed time away from their families.

Pam resisted asking the time again. "Do you think he will really believe any of this?"

"If he thinks he can get two women that look like us to bed free he'll believe damn near anything. We just can't afford to scare him off before we get our hooks set."

"You make him sound like a fish."

"He is a fish, a poor fish. Oh damn, here he comes."

Oddly enough, in the girls' opinion, Ned Breaker looked like his picture in the paper. A stocky five feet-eleven, thinning blond hair, and watery blue eyes. The constant flush in his face gave evidence of heavy drinking. He quickly surveyed the lounge. With no easy touches in sight he headed for an empty section of the bar. While he considered which cheap whiskey to order, Gabby slipped onto the stool next to his.

"Aren't you Ned Breaker with *The Review*?"

Breaker turned to face the intruder. Her wide brown eyes held his attention for only a second. Some fine body, he thought. "Yeah, what do you need this evening?"

Gabby turned slightly so she could nod her head at Pam, and also so Breaker got an even better look at her legs. "It's not for me. My friend wants to ask you a professional question."

"Professional? Let me guess what profession." Breaker thought to himself if there was a tariff, he wanted to know up front. No need to disappoint the girls later. "You gonna stand me to a drink?"

"If you'll drink it with us. My friend, JoAnne, works for a Baltimore paper. She's here on business. I tagged along so we can have some fun on the side. But she does have a serious question for you. You coming?"

Breaker turned to the bartender. "Double Glenlivet on

the rocks. Put it on the girls' tab and bring it over there."

Gabby slid from the bar stool and walked toward their table. Breaker followed. From her seat Pam could see the voluptuous sway of Gabby's hips. As if challenged, Pam crossed her legs revealing even more flesh.

"Mr. Breaker, this is my friend JoAnne Gorman."

"Hey, I thought we were buddies. Call me Ned."

"Yes sir, Mr. Breaker." They caught Pam's light humor and laughed. Breaker's drink arrived.

"What're you drinking, Ned?" Pam leaned toward Breaker as she spoke.

"Glenlivet, kid. Old Ned goes first class."

That part of what the woman at *The Review* told her was right on the money. Pam could feel her anxiety growing. *Maybe this thing is going to work.*

Breaker's thoughts were simpler. If this is a dream don't wake me up 'til it's over.

Pam shook her head when their bartender inquired about another round of drinks.

He returned to his station and moved down the bar next to a co-worker. "A fiver says those girls have Breaker out of here in ten minutes or less."

"Go away. I'll bet you a ten they can do it in less than five."

***

"Come on now, you said you'd tell." Pam wanted to sound firm, but not pushy.

Breaker took a sip from his third scotch. "It's just like I told you gals down in the bar, the way Ned Breaker plays, it's tit-for-tat. You want something good from me then I expect something good in return from you guys."

Breaker sat in the middle of a couch. Gabby leaned back against one arm with her shoeless feet in his lap. Pam sat facing them in an easy chair. The suite justified the price. A living area also contained a table suitable for a small meeting and a wet bar, now the home of a partially empty bottle of Glenlivet and a bottle of highly watered down wine. A door led to a bedroom with an adjoining bath.

"Come on now, rub my feet some more." Gabby purred. "I've told you that Ned Breaker won't go home hungry tonight. We're getting high and hot."

Instinctively Pam rolled her eyes to the ceiling.

Breaker killed his drink. "Look, get me another one. Tell me exactly want you want to know and let's get on with this. Get yourselves another one while you're at it."

Pam played hostess and then returned to her chair. She feared if he didn't open up soon, he would pass out. Breaker massaged Gabby's feet as he looked to Pam for an answer.

Pam frowned at her friend. *Dammit, she doesn't have to enjoy it that much. At least open your eyes. Oh God, what if Gabby falls asleep on me.*

"Look Ned, I can write, I've had a few by-lines, and in every case the editors liked my stuff. But I'll never make it unless I can get inside something and really kick up some dust." Pam began believing herself. "I need something like you did on that Andrews person in Mount Vernon. Honest, didn't you ever have a break before you became *The Review's* top columnist?"

Pam's open flattery paid off. "Anders, not Andrews. Actually I did. On Watergate with Woodard and Bernstein, I was pretty much their right-hand man through the investigation."

Pam grimaced. Yeah sure, Rick once told her Breaker was nothing but a gofer.

"After what we did on that I had pretty much a blank check, so I worked as a stringer for about five years. Great life, away from the editors, making your own rules, playing your own game." Breaker paused for another long sip. His right hand slid up the inside of Gabby's thigh until it stopped.

Gabby's eyes popped open. "Boy, we're getting frisky aren't we." She took Breaker's hand between hers as she pulled her legs under her. She put Ned's index finger in her mouth.

"Oh shit! What the hell are you doing! Dammit, let go!"

Gabby relaxed her teeth. "I just wanted to give you a preview of what's in store for later. I didn't hurt you did I baby?" Gabby faked a girlish pout.

"Bite on my dong like that and you'll kill me."

"Honest?"

"Will you two quit playing. You want hotel security up here? Ned, can you stay to the point now?"

He continued. "Okay, okay, back in March this guy calls me. I sort of know him. Steve Mo . . . Never mind that, he does import and export over in Silver Spring. Says he wants five grand for a hot story. I tell him no dice, maybe a grand and a little more later if it pans out. Take it or leave it. We end up at fifteen hundred with maybe up to two grand later, if his stuff is worth anything. I need another drink."

Pam handed him the drink. "Now talk before you pass out."

"Old Ned never passes out. Just wait you'll see. Where was I? Oh yeah, we meet and he tells me this story. 'Bout ten years ago he's over in Bangkok working for a guy named Rajah Khan. A Chinaman named Bill Lee is Khan's number one man. Khan has his finger in a lot of things. Drugs, white slavery, but his big operation's money laundering. Khan's a two-bit operator, but in those days with everything wide open he still turned more than a hundred million a year. Then the roof caved in. Don't know all the details, except that worldwide the lid clamped shut on the money business. The big players just cut back some, but the marginal players like Khan were getting killed." Breaker paused and drained most of his glass.

"Ned, hurry up and get to the point." Pam leaned forward and slid to the edge of chair.

"My guy went to Lee and told him that with his connections all over the world he thought he could move some dough. Lee was desperate and told my guy they would go with two hundred-fifty thousand if he thought he could handle it."

Breaker's head wove to and fro. Pam knew if he passed out all of their effort was for nothing. "Hey, Ned, you all right? You need to hurry up so the games can start. As soon as you finish I'll get you another drink."

"Nother drink, good idea."

"Talk first."

Breaker tried to frown at Pam, "Man you're one rough broad. Where was I . . . Yeah. My guy's sitting in the lounge at a five-star hotel in Bangkok when this Anders walks up. Anders says he knew him from Nam but he's working for AID now. Anders offers to help with moving some money. My guy says sure, fifty-fifty? Anders agrees. Now get this, here's the kind of person Anders is. He pushes my guy out and does it all on his own. Takes Lee's money to some place offshore. In a few days, five fifty-thousand dollar deposits appear in Khan's bank accounts all over the US. Slick as a whistle." Breaker's eyes slowly closed.

"That's not everything is it?" Pam asked.

"Come on, tell all," Gabby added, "or you get no goodies tonight."

Breaker winched when Gabby jabbed her extended

fingers under his rib cage. "Well just wait a minute. Let's see, then a bunch of stuff happens all at once. First Lee calls my guy in and tells him about when Khan and Lee worked in Nam they lost five million in a currency conversion. They weren't sure if Anders set them up or if he got duped himself. Either way, Lee had convinced Khan not to do any more business with Anders. Didn't matter 'cause Anders never came back to Bangkok anyway."

Pam jumped in her seat. For the first time she fully understood Breaker. Her father's last trip to Bangkok. "Go ahead Ned. It's starting to get good."

"Gets even better. Don't forget you still owe me a piece of Scotch. Lee tells him business is opening up again. Now Khan had moved out of Southeast Asia into Europe and mostly into North America. Lee wants my guy to go to DC and take over a little business they have in Maryland. Lee'll come over here later with all the details. They stake my guy to a cool twenty-five grand and he's off."

Breaker had his second wind, pausing only to nurse his drink. "Later Lee contacts my guy and says he's on his way to the US. He'll stop on his way to New York to meet him. Looks like Khan is spending time in New York. My guy waits, no Lee. Then he checks around and finds out that when Lee walked out of customs at San Francisco International the Feds nabbed him. Lee folded up like a wet towel and turned over the names of all Khan's key people in the US. Lee must'a cut a deal with the Feds."

While it appeared the part about her father had ended, Pam figured the rest of this might be valuable too. She sat with her eyes glued on Breaker, who continued.

"My guy waits for the law. They're picking up the rest of Khan's people left and right. But no knock on the door. He's having problems getting hold of Khan, but Khan sends him some money from time to time. He checked with AID, Anders had gone, didn't work there anymore. Then he reads in the paper that Anders and his old lady got wasted. He figures it's score settling time and he's probably on the list. After nine, ten months he's still alive and broke so he runs me down. There."

"That's it?"

"That's it. I want a drink and I've got to pee."

Pam fixed a full portion this time and after Gabby helped him to his feet, she handed the drink to Breaker. As Gabby lead Breaker to the bedroom, she looked back at Pam and winked. When the bedroom door closed Pam went into action. The Scotch and wine bottles went back into a portable bar. All fingerprints were wiped off the fixtures and shoes and purses gathered together. When Gabby returned, the girls took their belongings and left the room.

***

"Where did you leave Breaker?" Pam asked as she followed the flow of traffic back to Virginia and on to Springfield.

"Stark naked lying on top of the bedspread with his willie in his hand. Did any of what he said make sense to you?"

"Some of it. Daddy had something to do with a currency conversion, I don't know what. He worked for AID and he did make a last trip to Bangkok. He came back really proud of something he had done. Brought all kind of stuff. Big thing was an antique hemp wall hanging Mom put in the dining room. I'm certain the hotel was the Royal Bangkok and the lounge the Imperial Lounge."

"How do you know?"

"I heard Daddy talk about it."

"What's next?"

"I've got to find a Steve Mo somewhere in Silver Spring."

"You're going to keep digging into this?"

"I have to, Gabby, I have no choice. This was just a first step."

Gabby nodded her head, she understood.

CHAPTER 7
MORRIS I

Pam looked at the sheets of paper. The desk clock said ten forty. They both referred to this room as Rick's office, even though Pam spent as much time there as her husband. The cherry desk and burgundy leather chair had been purchased as a set. It combined taste, comfort, and function. Pam liked that combination. She and Rick might have differences, but not on things like this.

It had taken her less than two hours to go through the list, only two names to go. She referred to one of the sheets, reached for the phone and dialed.

"Yes, please. Could you tell me if Steve is in? You don't. Thank you anyway."

Pam hesitated. This was the last one. Between the import and export places she found in the phone book and the ones the Silver Spring Chamber faxed to her, there were twenty names. She guessed Ned was sharper than they thought. He had certainly sent her off on a wild goose chase. Of course three didn't answer. She decided to try them one more time after this last one.

"Yes ma'am, may I speak to Steve please. No, I don't believe he goes by any other name. Thank you. You have a nice day too."

Pam thumbed through the sheets, "Whoa, I forgot about this one, its line was busy twice. Maybe three's a lucky number." She dialed it again.

"Yes, may I speak to Steve please? You have two Steves? I'm not sure. What're their last names? No, not Steve Barton?" Pam could barely control her excitement. "Yes, Steve Morris, the owner, that's the one I want. Is he in?" The next few seconds lasted for hours. "Yes, Mr. Morris, excuse me, Steve. My name's Pam Wilson. No, you don't know me. We have some mutual friends from Bangkok who said I should look you up when I got to DC."

A very long pause. Obviously she had taken Steve Morris by surprise. "I really can't explain it over the phone. I wondered if we could have lunch Monday. We can cover it in a half hour or so. I understand your schedule and Silver Spring is fine. Do you know the Silver Flame? That's the one on Fenton down from Highway Four Ten. . . great. Is a late lunch okay, maybe one-thirty? Good, I'll see you there Monday at one-thirty. Yes, you have a nice weekend too."

Pam swung around in the swivel chair with her eyes closed.

"I cannot believe this. I need to get with Gabby and figure out how to approach Morris."

***

"There's something I need to tell you before you leave this morning, Rick."

"Monday morning's the wrong time to give your husband bad news." Rick continued to stare at *The Review*.

"I'm getting an implant today, what size boobs should I go for?"

Rick lowered the paper. He looked stern. "If you think

we can afford to replace all of your bras, you're crazy. What do you want? Look, paper down, undivided attention."

"Do you remember when you went to Philly last week?"

"Uh-huh."

"Well, while you were gone, Gabby and I saw Breaker. He wasn't all that happy, but he saw us. Maybe he got tired of the phone calls. While he talked, he dropped the name of his informer for the story about Daddy."

"Why did you take Gabby?"

"Safety in numbers I guess."

"I'm sorry sweetheart, but I cannot, in my wildest possible dreams, imagine Ned Breaker ever doing that."

"Okay. Maybe we used some of our feminine charms and maybe he got hot for Gabby. The guy's name is Steve Morris. He's in the import export business in Silver Spring. Do you know him?"

"Pamela, this area has over one million people in it. I doubt if I know two hundred of 'em, and I sure as hell know very few connected with double homicides. You're asking for trouble if you go see this guy."

"You don't know that."

"Don't know which? If he's a murderer or if you're asking for trouble? The first one depends on a trial and a verdict. The second one's simple, if you go to lunch with this guy you're asking for trouble."

"I'm sorry, Rick. I never should have sprung this on you, but I was afraid you'd get angry, so I put off telling you. This Morris has nothing to do with the murders. He knew Daddy in Bangkok and told Breaker some things. I just want to find out if what Breaker wrote had any relation to what Morris told him."

"Interesting idea. So you think maybe Breaker picked up a couple of crumbs and shot a few times from the hip to see what might happen. Like I said, interesting, but Pam, I flat do not want you seeing that guy."

Color raised in Pam's cheeks, her jaw was set and her nostrils flared. The Wilsons stared at each other. *I love him, but he can be the most obstinate ass in the world.*

Rick's thoughts took a different vein. Pam never realized how beautiful she looked when angry. Rick knew he would lose the argument. His concern was for her safety. Why did she have to be so damn stubborn?

"Of course if you forbid me to go, well, that's something else."

"Look, don't be like this. I don't own you and I can't forbid you to do anything. But I am your husband and entitled to be concerned over my wife's safety. If you go, please keep your wits about you. Don't do anything careless. And remember if you're not sure, cut and run. Agreed?"

"Okay. You don't really think I'd walk down a dark alley with this guy do you?" Pam smirked as she reached for her coffee.

"Don't try to make me laugh. You wanted to talk to Breaker and find out where his crap came from. Right?"

Pam nodded.

"You have that. Now come hell or high water you're going to see what's his name Morris. Right?"

Another nod.

"You do realize there's an excellent chance he won't even talk to you? After you've seen this guy, can you drop it there?"

Pam knew Rick would get around to that, and she hated to lie to him again if she could avoid it.

"Hey, look at the time, you've got to get going or you'll hit the worst of rush hour. We can talk some more tonight"

Pam's gaze followed Rick from the room. She understood his concern for her safety and his open objection to her actions. Pam realized if she was to pursue this she must continue keeping Rick in the dark.

***

Traffic crossing the Potomac on the Arlington Memorial Bridge crawled giving Pam time to think. She knew Rick was worried, and she needed to be careful what she told him. Gabby and Rick had both warned her that Morris probably would not want to talk to her. Gabby was right, she needed one very strong play to hit Morris with.

I may have only one chance. If I slip, he'll walk.

She navigated around the Lincoln Memorial and took 23rd Street toward Highway 29. She knew this would not be like Breaker. All they needed there was a cover story that didn't sound too bad and then just keep throwing booze and sex at him. Morris will be different. This time she had no idea what to expect or how to approach him. Pam eased into the traffic on Highway 29, thirty minutes from the restaurant.

Traffic now moved in cadence with the changing lights. Pam's mind drifted back to her senior year at Mount Vernon Senior High. She was painfully shy and to her debating, being forced to stand and talk in public, seemed a perfect answer. As captain, her Mount Vernon team won debate after debate. Finally, in early May, they represented northern Virginia in the state finals facing the perennial champion from Richmond.

The issue that year was, "Should the United States Formally Recognize Red China, Pro or Con." Pam drew the con position for her team. The rules were simple. Four debaters alternating presentations, with a summary by the team captains. Pro went first.

For the first time all year they faced a team as capable as they were. Well prepared, poised, and articulate. It came down to the captains. While every team that argued pro had stressed the economics of recognition, he carried it a step further. "If each of the one billion Chinese bought just one dollar's worth of US goods each day, and the income tax on the resulting corporate profits put into a special fund . . . the National Debt could be paid off in one lifetime." His presentation received a nice round of applause. He graciously thanked everyone and sat down.

Pam covered her usual con points. Where the next words came from she never knew, they simply appeared in her mouth.

"Those who support recognition of Red China paint that country's Communist government as open and benevolent. They never tell you of the five hundred thousand Chinese citizens who have died, who have been murdered, for opposing a Communist dictatorship. We should not, no, we must not, sell the souls of a half a million martyrs for a Coke© and a Big Mac©."

Pam had spoken her last few words standing on tiptoe, leaning over the podium, each word punctuated by a jab of her right forefinger toward the audience.

A few claps sounded in the hall, then more and more. After deliberations that seemed to last for hours, Mount Vernon Senior High School was declared the state champion.

They had won all of their debates during the year, so Pam walked to the podium knowing exactly what to say. She looked down at her parents in the front row. Her grinning father had his right fist in front of his chest. As Pam watched, his thumb stuck straight in the air. Thumbs up from her father. She knew she had done well.

That day, twenty years ago, words appeared in her mouth when she needed them. She wasn't sure how, but she knew it would happen like that again today.

CHAPTER 8
MORRIS II

Pam's mind leaped back to the present. She had driven in a near trance and was now only minutes from her destination. She turned left onto Fenton toward The Silver Flame. Past the restaurant was a parking lot; she pulled in.

Pam walked two doors back to the restaurant, the plate glass front proclaimed, "Steaks, Chops, and Maryland Seafood." To the left of the door was a menu covered with a sheet of thick plastic. Above the menu, behind another sheet of plastic rested a faded hand written note:

I personally guarantee you will have a good meal.
Dimitrios

Pam entered, the aroma of Middle Eastern spices assailed her senses. Outwardly the Silver Flame mirrored a thousand other restaurants in Metro DC. Fifteen or so tables, each with a white linen cloth, a salt and pepper mill, a tray of sugar and sweeteners, and an artificial flower in a cheap glass vase. In rural America this would be called something like Lulu's Café, and have the best food in the county. Here, if the food didn't live up to Dimitrios' promise, it would go out of business. Too much competition.

Curly black hair, brown eyes, and a wide toothy white smile greeted Pam.

"Yes Ma'am?"

"You have reservations for Wilson? I'm expecting a gentleman to join me."

"Yes Ma'am." He led her to a table near the door with a perfect view of the street.

"We'll be talking business, could we have that one against the side wall?"

"Yes Ma'am." He pulled out a chair and handed her a menu. "My name is Nick. I'm your server today."

Pam declined hearing the day's specials She did inquire as to the ladies room. With a smile Nick pointed to the rear of the restaurant. When Pam looked in that direction, she saw a neon sign reading, "Restrooms."

After touching up her makeup, Pam returned to the restaurant. Her watch said one twenty-eight. She checked out the room. Late, but still a few people eating. The decor was Mediterranean. She looked at the menu. Tuna salad sandwich, a dumb thing to order in a Greek restaurant, but all she wanted and probably would not even eat that. Pam looked up with a start.

The man who just walked in must be Steve Morris. He spoke to Nick who nodded and led the stranger toward Pam. As they walked toward her table, she checked out Morris. Late fifties at least, thinning brown hair, blue eyes, six feet maybe, easily a couple hundred pounds. His khaki slacks and open neck shirt were rumpled, it appeared his shoes had never been defaced with polish. He hadn't shaved today, maybe not yesterday either.

Pam stood up. She hoped her navy suit, cream blouse, and navy pumps made her look important and not like an old maid librarian. She had added a ruby and sapphire pin depicting a Thai dancing girl under the correct assumption that had she lived in Thailand she would have bought one.

"Mrs. Wilson, I'm Steve Morris of Global Imports. How are you today?"

"Fine. I'm glad you could join me for lunch."

"Sure, got to eat lunch anyhow. You ordered yet?"

"Not yet"

"Best thing's the jumbo hamburger. Meal all by itself. How about a drink?" Before Pam could answer, he waved to Nick. "Sam Adams Light."

Nick looked at Pam who shook her head.

"They say Sam Adams was a real trouble maker, a rabble-rouser that started a war not everybody wanted. But that old boy sure makes fine beer. Light for lunch, dark for dinner." Nick brought the beer. Morris drank a third of the bottle in one swallow.

Pam averted her eyes from Morris and hoped he wouldn't belch. Morris belched. "Okay lady what can I do you for? If it's drugs, forget it, if it's more jewelry like you got on, I can get you a price that'll knock your . . . ah . . . socks off."

Pam was developing an enormous dislike for Mr. Morris.

"Let's order, you're buying, you asked me out you know."

"Sure," Pam replied.

Nick returned and while they ordered, Morris finished his beer. Nick brought another one. A third of that one immediately disappeared.

"Let's get going. Call me Steve."

This was it. "Steve, my full name is Pam Anders Wilson. I'm Bill and Betty Anders daughter. I want to talk to you about what you told Ned Breaker concerning my late father."

Since childhood Steve Morris had a tic in his eyes when he came under stress. Both eyes involuntarily blinked as he stood up. "Look lady, I don't know what the hell your game is, or what you think you're after, but let me tell you straight off, I don't know any Bill Anders, any Ned Breaker, or any other crap you can dream up. You got that. I'm outta here!"

Pam's face glowed crimson, her jaw set. Fortunately Morris couldn't see under the table. Pam's knees shook. She knew she had one shot and it had to be good.

"Look you son-of-a-bitch. You have two choices. You can sit down and talk to me or I'm going to the Feds with what I know about your dealings with Rajah Khan and Bill Lee. And very honestly Steve, I couldn't give a damn less if your ass rots in Leavenworth for the next twenty years."

Steve Morris was stunned. Women didn't talk back to him. This sexy little brunette he planned hitting on later talked to him like a longshoreman. And even worst, he strongly suspected she was dead serious. Eyes now going crazy, Morris' mouth opened and closed as he tried to think of something to say.

Pam thought he looked like a goldfish out of water.

Morris turned to follow Pam's eyes. Nick and an older man, maybe Dimitrios, were standing by the front door. They watched without smiling. With a sigh of resignation, Morris picked up his beer and finished it in one very long, loud swallow. He pointed to the empty bottle and held up a finger. The other two men looked at each other. The older one nodded. Still watching them, Nick went to the bar and Morris sat down.

"Okay, what do you want?"

"I want to know what you know, what went on in Vietnam, what went on in Bangkok, and what went on in Mount Vernon. All of it pertaining to my father."

"I thought you'd talked to Breaker?"

"I have, but what he told me and what you told him are probably not the same."

"Boy, you really do know that asshole don't you. You know that SOB still owes me two grand. Next time you see him, remind him. Okay."

Their lunch arrived and Morris began talking as he ate. "Steve Morris will do most anything for a buck, always have, but I draw the line at drugs and murder. Believe me, lady, I had nothing to do with your folks getting killed."

This came from a man who looked as though he slapped women around when he could get away with it. Now he whined like a little kid, begging for something.

"Go on."

"I went to Breaker 'cause I was short on cash, I mean broke. Otherwise I would never blab about things I know need to be kept quiet. From time to time Khan sends me some cash and a little work, but not enough. Global makes a few bucks but that's all."

"I understand." Pam had no idea what he was talking about.

Steve continued working on his jumbo burger as he talked. "Now I do have some ideas about what happened to your folks. I'll tell you about them later. In Bangkok your father said he knew me in Nam, which wasn't true. I think he had somebody in the bar point me out.

"I did know his name. A couple of guys with the US Government said he almost caused some real trouble for them. They were into stuff they wouldn't want their mothers or their bosses to know about. Anders gets sent back to the states, some other guy takes his place but nothing happens."

That must have been when we went to Pennsylvania.

"Later, Bill Lee tells me how Khan lost more than five million dollars in an MPC currency conversion. Lee believed Anders had set them up, Khan thought Anders had been used. The bad part from Khan and Lee's point of view is that with the black market and the way we propped up the South Vietnamese economy, given nine months or so, they could have made maybe twenty million, some real money."

Morris stopped talking and looked at an empty beer bottle.

"I'm getting dry."

Everyone else had left the restaurant. Nick sat on a bar stool watching them. One nod from Morris and Nick slid from the stool and moved back to work.

"In Bangkok I did some odd jobs for Khan and Lee. Ten, fifteen years ago drug money moved all over the world, wide open. Developing countries' financial systems and economies were getting real shaky. There was talk of a big international collapse if places like Singapore, Jakarta, or maybe Rio bellied up and defaulted on billions of dollars in loans to the big US, European, and Japanese banks. All of the banking and international police organizations got together and shut down most of the money flow. The big cartels slowed up but kept trucking. The little fish like Khan were getting wiped out.

"After a decade in Southeast Asia, I've got quite a few connections. I go to Lee and offer to help out. He says they need a quarter million moved quick. After three weeks I'm dead in the water. Nothing. One afternoon I'm sitting in the Royal Bangkok Hotel drowning my sorrows."

"That was the Imperial Lounge?" Pam held her breath. Had she overplayed her hand on this one?

Morris looked surprised. "Oh yeah, I guess you would know that place. What you wouldn't know about are the places where I usually hung out."

"No, and I don't think I really want to know either."

Morris laughed over another bite of jumbo hamburger. "Fine. We'll drop all that." He continued. "Like I said,

Anders walks up. He's with AID. You know what that is?"

"Yes."

"Knows all about the money. I've talked to so many people about it I don't pay any attention. Says he has a group that can take care of it. I ask him if he would split. Sure, he says. Hate to tell you Pam, but your father lied. I get him with Lee, and wham, I'm out in the cold. To make it short, Anders pulled it off."

"How much more do you have? It's three o'clock."

"One more beer and fifteen minutes."

Pam nodded agreement.

"Lee calls me in. Anders had turned a quarter million of dirty money into five clean fifty-thousand dollar deposits to Khan's accounts in North America.. Anders had gone back to the States, Lee didn't think he would return."

Pam frowned. *That damned last trip to Bangkok again.*

"But they have decided not to do any more business with him anyway. The heat's off and they can take care of themselves now. Then Lee lets me in on the real stuff. Khan has moved out of Asia with his big work. He has some of it in Europe, but the bulk moved to North America. Khan has a whole floor in Manhattan with just his New York people. They want me to come here and open up Global. Lee said he would come later to explain everything. I get some seed money and I'm outta there. In a couple months Lee calls international, says he will be in Dulles the next week on flight so-and-so. I go to Dulles to meet my boss. No Lee. I wait a few days and call Khan's office in New York. Khan's not there but I tell them who I am and that I'm looking for Bill Lee. See, I figured Lee must have gone to Manhattan first."

Pam was becoming overwhelmed. She knew she would not remember even a third of this and would have given anything for a tape recorder. She looked at her plate. The tuna salad sandwich and chips had disappeared.

"Well. I'll tell you the shit hit the fan. New York thought he was with me and they were sore 'cause he hadn't called them yet. I start checking around. I've got this buddy who has informed for the FBI and has a few ins. He tells me that when Lee walked out of customs in San Francisco the Feds hit him. He didn't know what they threatened Lee with, but he caved in and cut a deal. Lee got a new name and a few years of soft time."

Pam's eyebrows went up.

Morris leaned back in his chair. He seemed, for the first time, to relax. "That means minimum security, some folks call them country clubs with bars."

"What did Lee give the Feds?"

"Only a complete list of all of Khan's key people in North America. The moron had his address book in his suitcase. They were already getting picked up. Shit, I figured this was it. Several years later I'm still here. Only one problem, I'm just getting by with an underfinanced business and an occasional handout from Khan. Then one day I pick up the paper and see where your folks were murdered. Somebody tried to make it look like a bunch of junkies. No, I believe pros made it look that way. Not sure I can tell you why I think that, but I do. I figured it was pay back time, and since the Feds missed me, I must be on this list. Again a year goes by and I'm still alive. Alive, but broke as hell. That's when I had to go see Breaker."

They sat in silence for a few minutes. What is there to say now? Steve had really opened up. Was it all true? Pam believed so. She wished just one person would tell her something that she could not tie together in her mind, then maybe she could have some doubts about her father's activities back then.

"Thank you Steve. I appreciate your openness. I want you to know that everything you have told me is in strict confidence."

"Sure. You get to New York often?"

"Sometimes."

"Well look, tell Khan or his boys that Steve Morris needs some more work."

"Be more than happy to do that."

Morris stood up. "Got to get back to my place. See ya around."

"Good bye and again thank you."

Morris turned back. "I guess you already know this but that private number of Khan's is a joke; leave a message and only once in a while will they ever return it."

"What do you do?" Pam couldn't believe her ears.

"I just call the regular number."

"What's it listed under now?"

"It's still Swiss Trading Company. Don't forget to say something to Khan about me."

"Don't worry, I will."

Morris turned and walked from the restaurant.

Pam paid the check, called Gabby, and left a message for Rick that she was still alive. She got away from the restaurant just ahead of rush hour traffic.

Driving home, she spoke out loud. "Well Daddy, did I get a thumbs up again today?"

***

The light blinked on his unlisted telephone. They all had this number, but only two of them ever used it.

"Hello."

"You alone?"

"Yeah."

"We may have a problem of sorts."

"Such as?"

"You know that Anders kid?"

"You mean Pam Wilson?"

"Yeah, she's been sucking around Morris."

"How'd she find him."

"Breaker ran his stupid mouth."

"How do you know?"

"The tap's still on Steve's phone. We listen some."

"That damn jerk. What do you want done?"

"Keep your eyes and ears open. Morris was poor mouthing it again. Send him five hundred, no . . . no, make it twenty-five hundred. Put a note with the money calling it an advance on some work. When he's broke, he talks too damned much."

"Send it from New York?"

"Of course."

"Anything else?"

The line went dead. The caller had hung up.

CHAPTER 9
KHAN

Information had supplied the Swiss Trading Company's telephone number, but Pam did not get an answer until nine thirty Tuesday morning.

"May I speak to Mr. Rajah Khan please?"

"Mr. Khan not here now. Who call please?" The voice sounded Filipino.

"Would you tell Mr. Khan that someone who knew him in Bangkok is coming to New York and would like to come by the office and say hello?"

"Name please."

"Mr. Khan knew me as Piper DuVal. We got together at the Royal Bangkok Hotel a couple of times. I think he will remember me when you tell him."

The line went silent a few minutes. "You call back tomorrow. I ask Mr. Khan. My name Phillip. Good bye."

Hours drug slowly until the next morning when she called New York again. "Phillip, this is Miss DuVal. Have you had a chance to talk to Mr. Khan?"

"Yes, Missy. When you come New York? Mr. Khan say he want see you again."

"What about tomorrow morning? Say eleven thirty?"

"All good."

"Look, I'm coming on the shuttle from DC. I could easily run late."

"Eleven thirty, twelve thirty all same. Mr. Khan here."

They exchanged good byes.

***

Thursday morning Pam stood in her living room, peering through tilted blinds at a group of twelve children in a queue waiting to board their school bus. As they had done for the past two weeks, Ricky and Adam directed the other children into a line. Smallest children in front, largest ones in the back, girls before boys by age group. While Ricky and Adam were hardly the oldest, none of the other children questioned the boys' directions. She was not allowed outside the house before the bus came. "Mother, pleeease!" Even Rick had to stay hidden. Pam had no idea why she wanted Rick or herself watching until Ricky safely boarded his bus except that he was still her baby.

The bus left and Pam walked toward the back of the house. The summer program proved fantastic. Instead of Ricky and Adam being the new kids in school this fall, they would already have a group of friends and know their way around school. Three weeks ago he was wetting his bed and about to be expelled from the program. She hummed to herself as she continued to the kitchen where Rick thumbed through a legal file.

"Eat your breakfast. You know your blood sugar level will go to zero by mid-morning if you don't eat a good breakfast?"

"Huh?"

"It's stone cold. Give me your plate. You can have my bacon, I'll make some more eggs and toast. In the meantime please tell me what you're doing?"

Pam turned her back and went to work on another meal. Maybe it was because of her father, or maybe ancestors a million years ago, but she loved to see her mate completely focused. In some unexplained way it made her feel safe.

"We have the final preliminary meetings on the merger today and tomorrow. Seems like every day I'm getting more and more of it to handle."

"That's good isn't it? Over or scrambled?"

"Either."

"Good 'cause I just broke a yolk. Scrambled it is. Seriously, getting such a big role in something like this helps your career doesn't it?"

"Sure. If this works and the merger comes off, I'm certainly on track to make partner. If not this year, maybe next year."

Pam brought Rick his second breakfast. "Eat! And tell me more about it. You never have you know."

"Okay. Until recently I had not seen the whole package. Now that I'm coordinating all of our effort, it's almost over-whelming. The Canadian firm has the basic technology and even better products on the drawing board, but lack the resources to do anything with them. The Japanese firm has a super team of people to market, distribute, and support the product worldwide. Our client has a high-tech electronics manufacturing capability that may be the best in the world. This is the biggest thing the O'Dell firm has handled in over ten years."

"This sounds like a merger made in heaven. I'd think everybody would be working together on it."

"They are. But when you get something as big as Microsoft, even with everyone on board, a lot must be compromised and settled. I can't lie though. It's a hell of a lot of fun."

"What happens if it doesn't go together?"

"I'll get a good pair of Nikes and chase ambulances. I'm going to be late getting home tonight, so I'll catch dinner in town. What have you got on for today?"

"I'm going to take the shuttle to New York and do some book stuff for Lindsey. I should get back well before five. Ricky's going to Adam's after school."

"Could you explain why Lindsey doesn't take the shuttle to New York while you watch the store for her?"

"You men, you're always making things complicated. Hurry or you'll never get to work."

***

Pam leaned her seat back as best she could. The 737's on the shuttle were cramped even for someone no larger than her. If they arrived on time, she should make eleven thirty. Chat with Khan a while. Maybe get taken to lunch. Catch the three o'clock back home. Piece of cake. This was really different than meeting Morris. Khan's looking forward to seeing her, and this time she had a neat little cover story.

Pam considered her story a work of art. Gabby agreed it was so stupid that it had to be true. Pam was Piper, who in her early twenties worked for several years as a *fille de joie* in Amsterdam and The Hague. During that time she went to Bangkok for a few months where she met Mr. Khan. She was quite certain Khan had met enough women in Bangkok he could not remember them all. Piper now lives in Chicago and on a visit to DC met a friend of a friend named Pam Wilson who told her Pam's late father, Bill Anders, had once worked for Mr. Khan. Pam wanted Piper to ask Khan if he knew anything about what happened to Pam's father and mother. They were both killed about a year ago.

What this might bring from Khan, Pam had no idea. But

she even had a plan in the event Khan wanted her to go back to "work" for the evening. Make the date and then get on the shuttle home.

***

Pam gave the cabbie a twenty and a ten and waved away the change. She turned and looked at 745 Allen Street. From the molded iron facade, the building appeared to date from before the First World War. Inside, the small lobby of black and mauve marble indicated a twenties or thirties renovation. A directory listed tenants by floor. The Swiss Trading Company shared the fourteenth floor with eight other businesses.

Pam stopped before suite 1404. Stale cigarette smoke mingled with musty carpet created an unpleasant odor. In New York fashion the door had a key pad, a buzzer, and a one-way peep hole. She pressed the buzzer. The door swung open to reveal a short Filipino. "Ah, Miss DuVal?"

"Yes. We've talked. You're Phillip?"

"Please come in and sit down, I get Mr. Khan."

He ushered Pam into a reception area approximately twenty feet by twenty feet. Phillip motioned toward two chairs separated by a small table. On the facing wall stood a sofa table with an arrangement of artificial flowers. A mirror was mounted on the wall behind the table. A wooden desk and chair, probably Phillip's, faced the hall. A door behind the desk was the only other exit from the office. Phillip disappeared through that portal. Pam sat in one of the side chairs.

Well, here is little Pam Wilson getting ready to chat with a well-known international criminal, or whatever Breaker called him. Pam could not resist a smile.

Phillip returned holding a eight by ten inch photograph.

"Mr. Khan want know if you remember any these people?"

Pam suspected a trap. She had no idea what Khan looked like, how could she possibly pick him out of a group photograph. Pam nonchalantly took the picture. The glossy print glared in the florescent lighting, but obviously Khan was not in it. A dozen or so oriental girls stood in front of what appeared to be an office building. On one side were two young Caucasian men. Pam carefully moved the print around.

"Phillip, I really can't recognize anyone. This girl does look sort of familiar. But you know it's been a few years and this photograph isn't all that sharp."

She handed the print back to Phillip, who took it carefully by the edges.

"I come back." He slipped out the door again.

Pam sat back down. Somewhere in the canyons of lower Manhattan a siren wailed. After several minutes she reached for a magazine on the end table. It did not surprise her that the leading British business magazine, *The Economist,* was in Khan's office. The date surprised her, February, 2004. She looked closer at the table and saw it was covered with dust, lots of it. So were the other magazines and the other chair. It appeared the office had not been used for months.

More time passed. She wondered if they were playing some type of mind games with her. Pam stood up and crossed to the sofa table. Still more dust. She looked at her watch. Phillip had been gone over twenty minutes. Pam opened her purse and took out a makeup bag. She may as well do something to kill time. Anyway Piper would definitely always look like a million dollars. Makeup finished, Pam adjusted her hair with her fingers. Then she gasped. Something had moved inside the mirror. It moved again looking like a shadow behind the glass. Then the mirror was still. Pam debated: bolt and run, or wait it out. She chose the latter and sat back down on her dusty chair.

Phillip finally reappeared and walked in front of her. She stood facing him.

"So sorry Missy, Mr. Khan no stay today. You leave now."

Phillip took her left arm above the elbow, turned her toward the door, and began walking with Pam in tow. Pam realized resistance would be futile. Phillip stopped and opened the door to the hall.

"Good bye. Mr. Khan he say thanks for coming."

"When will I get to see Mr. Khan? Should I call you again in a few days?"

"You go now, thank you very much."

The door closed with a metallic click. Pam felt her face flush as she turned on her heel and left the building.

***

Seated again in a 737 Pam's mind wandered. She knew she had hit a brick wall today. Why did they bring her to New York to jerk her around and play peeping tom? And the worst, from Pam's point of view, this was her last lead. She knew no more now than before she saw Breaker.

She looked out the window at clouds. With eyes half closed Pam remembered her first airplane trip.

She must have been five years old. The family was being transferred to somewhere in Pennsylvania. Before the move they flew to Tyler, Texas to see Betty's family: her parents, Grandmother and Grandfather Curtis, her older sister Donna, who came down from St. Louis, and her younger brother Chuck who still lived at home. Betty said Chuck was trying to find himself. Chuck said he was a hippie. To Pam, he represented the coolest thing she had ever seen. And there were cousins and cousins, and also

Betty's closest friend, Gloria.

Gloria's brother Ned, years earlier had come home on Thanksgiving leave from the Army. He brought with him a friend who had no place to go for the holidays. Saturday after Thanksgiving, the family had a party for the men. Gloria, of course, invited Betty. There Betty Curtis met Captain Bill Anders. Her two year old career as a school teacher was forgotten and in four months they married. Sixty days later Bill left the States for his first tour in Vietnam.

As young as she was, on this trip Pam realized the difference between her mother's family and her father's. Her father had no family. His parents had been killed in an automobile accident before his seventh birthday. His mother's family lived in Kansas. If Bill knew them it was only by name. Likely none of them had ever set foot in Texas. His father's only living relative was an older sister Ella. After his parents died, Bill went to live with Ella and her husband Al Davis in Lufkin, Texas. By any measure Al Davis was a good and hard working man, but at his best he barely made a living. Nor did they have the warm and happy life Bill had known with his parents. Al, Ella, and Bill shared a scraped out existence.

Even though Bill Anders spent most of his time in high school working, he graduated on the honor roll and starred on the local football team. Most area colleges recruited him, but when he set foot on the Texas A&M campus he knew that was where he belonged. The relaxed camaraderie of the cadets replaced the family he no longer had. In college his work ethic continued. He graduated third in his class and co-captained the football team. From his first semester in ROTC he had no doubt in his mind he would be an Army officer. Ella and Al both died before he graduated.

Pam jolted awake as the plane bounced into its' final approach to Reagan National Airport. She rubbed her eyes and checked the time. Pam watched Washington, DC pass beneath the airplane. *At least I won't be late getting home. Rick and I are going to the Vice President's party Saturday night. After that I'll think of something else to do. I'm not finished.*

***

A week later it hit Steve Morris. He sat upright in bed. "That Wilson dame who was going to throw my butt into prison didn't know any of that stuff until I sat there and ran my dumb mouth."

His secretary/girlfriend rolled over. "For cripes sake, shut up and go back to sleep. She got twenty-five hundred out of Khan for you, didn't she? What more do you want?"

CHAPTER 10
THE PARTY

"Damn, there must be six people ahead of us," Rick fumed.

A line of cars waited to pull in front of a brownstone down the street. They slowly crept forward.

"Thank you again, sweetheart."

"Uh-huh, for what?"

"Not getting upset over how much I paid for this dress. It's not every day a girl gets to go to a party with the vice-president of the United States. Anyway, it's a classic LBD that I'll wear to a lot of different affairs."

"LBD?"

Pam giggled. "Little black dress, I've told you that before."

They inched forward one car length.

"How about VELBD?"

"What?"

"Very expensive little black dress."

"Hey, I just gave you an atta-boy for not carping about the cost and you go and say that. Why not, very elegant little black dress?"

Only two cars remained in front of them.

"Monday at the office everybody will want to know what you talk about at a vice president's party? They won't believe what I tell them. Oh! I almost forgot. Guess what's going around DC now?"

They were one car back, but stopped and waiting.

"I haven't the foggiest."

"Your old buddy Ned Breaker got rolled by two hookers from Omaha, or somewhere out there. He claims they drugged him and lifted about a thousand dollars."

Gabby told Pam he had only fourteen dollars. "Do you think he'll press charges?"

"Probably not, going to a hotel room with prostitutes is sort of against the law."

"We're next if those people will ever get out of their car." Pam desperately wanted to change the subject.

But Rick kept talking. "One of the bartenders remembers the girls though. They hung out for a while waiting for Breaker then moved in on him. Place was so busy he didn't get a great description, but called one of them a good-looking Latino girl and the other one a mousy brunette."

Pam jerked in her seat. *Mousy brunette my ass.*

"Good they're moving now. What's bugging you all of a sudden?"

"Not one damn thing!"

By the time Rick pulled to the curb, put a claim check in his shirt pocket, and walked around the car to Pam, she was smiling.

"Boy it's not very often you have valet parking at someone's party. You okay now?"

"Sorry. The mention of Breaker just bugs me."

They walked up a few steps to the door. Two Marines in dress uniform flanked the doorway. When Pam and Rick approached them, the Marines snapped to attention. Inside a twenty-something in a dark suit directed them. "Right here, please."

They faced an older man with a high forehead, thick glasses, a pinched mouth and, of course, a dark suit. "Good evening, glad you could join us. Your names?"

"Pamela and Richard Wilson."

He turned to his left facing a man Pam vaguely recognized from network news. The vice president's something or other.

"Pamela and Richard Wilson."

Next in line was Vice President Goff, even more impressive in real life than on TV. Six feet three, graying temples, steel rimmed glasses, and a smooth tan that seemed to glow.

"Mrs. Wilson, Pamela. I'm so glad you could make it. Please make yourself at home and have a good time." As he spoke, he pivoted a quarter turn to his left. Pam's hand passed to the blond woman standing next to him. "Pamela Wilson, Dolly Goff."

"Oh Pamela, what a darling dress. You must tell me where you found it. We're so glad you could join us tonight. If there's anything you need, please tell one of the waiters."

Pam mumbled, "Thank you, Mrs. Goff."

Dolly Goff pivoted to her left. She released Pam's hand and turned back toward her husband. What happened next caught Pam by surprise.

"Richard Wilson!" Dolly Goff shrieked. "I wasn't sure if you could make it tonight or not. Oh, you can't believe how utterly thrilled I am that you took the time to come to one of our little parties. And this darling creature must be your wife."

Dolly's hand shot out and grabbed Pam's wrist pulling her back to Rick's side.

"Pamela, that's right isn't it? You are the luckiest lady

in the world to have the most brilliant lawyer in Washington for a husband." Trevor Goff drove his elbow into Dolly's side. "Well I must see to other guests. You two have a marvelous time and talk to me some more later."

They were released as Dolly, turning back toward her husband, said, "Why darling, I am so glad you could join us tonight."

As the Wilsons left the receiving line a waiter appeared, took their drink order, and disappeared. Pam surveyed the room which was, in fact, the entire bottom floor of the brownstone. Columns were spaced around the room and lush potted plants broke it into smaller areas. Fine art filled the walls and lavish oriental carpets covered the floor.

Pam faced her husband. "Before we mingle, I've got two questions."

"Shoot."

"I've been inside a lot of these Georgetown brownstones, but I have never seen one like this. It's been gutted, no walls, no nothing. How come?"

"Exceptionally astute question. When Goff was a senator, fifteen years worth, they bought two of these brownstones. This one and the one next door. As you put it, they gutted this one. See all the columns. They hold up the ceiling. Upstairs they can seat about fifty people for dinner, and have two more small rooms that'll seat fifteen each. They used this unit for parties and lived in the other one until the Blair House had a vacancy. Now they split their time between these two places and the Blair House."

"How do you know all this?"

Rick laughed. "One of the senior partners briefed me so if anyone asked, I had a very knowledgeable answer."

"I certainly hope I've made your evening." Pam waved across the room. "There's Mr. Timmons."

"The banker your dad worked for?"

"Uh-huh."

"Do you want to go over and say hi?"

"No." Pam replied. "He's talking to someone and I still have another question."

Their drinks arrived accompanied by another waiter carrying a tray of hors d'oeuvres.

"Good grief, caviar! Okay, what is it with Dolly? I thought she was going to wrap you up and take you home with her."

"Let's get over here, out of the way." Rick guided Pam next to a column. "Dolly owns an apartment house over in Reston, along with a lot of other property. Several months ago two young couples had been out drinking beer on a Saturday afternoon. On the way back to their car, one of the girls stepped on a broken piece of sidewalk in front of Dolly's place, fell down, and broke her ankle."

"Ouch. Was she hurt bad?"

"Not really. She had a clean break, no pin or anything like that."

"Dolly's fault?"

"Yes. The sidewalk's actually on her property. Some ambulance chaser got hold of the girl and they sued Dolly for two and a half million dollars."

"Good Lord, did she have insurance?"

"Yes, but not nearly that much. Maybe half a million. Dolly didn't want to use her husband's attorneys and somebody recommended us. Believe it or not, of all the partners and senior attorneys, I was the only one who had any real experience with personal liability cases. The time I spent with the Bartelle firm paid off, I must have handled a dozen cases.

"Anyway, I set up a meeting with the girl's attorney in one of the small conference rooms at our place. I had files all over the table. The guy came in, I'll call him Joe. We chatted, then Mr. Goldman, the number two partner came in, looked through a couple of files, nodded his head, went 'hummmm', and said, 'Richard, if you need any assistance on this call me.'

"He stared at Joe for a few seconds and then walked out. I honestly thought Joe would slide out of his chair he got so scared. We batted it back and forth for a while. I told him about the affidavits we had from the bar and how much his client drank, but that Mrs. Goff wanted to play fair. I offered three hundred thousand plus all medical costs."

"That sounds reasonable."

"It was. In court, a drunk falling down's not a strong case. But of course the Goffs had no desire to go to court under any circumstances. Joe said his client wouldn't agree to that, but maybe she would take four-fifty. I said I thought I could sell that, why don't you call your client. He said fine. I took him to a visitor's office to use the phone. I left, closed the door and went over to Matty's desk. The visitor's room phone goes through her station."

"Matty, your secretary?"

"Uh-huh. The light went on, Joe had made a call. In about thirty, forty seconds it went out. He had called time-of-day, his answering service, or something like that. He waited a few minutes longer for effect, then came out and said his client agreed."

"Well good for you, I guess."

"Yeah. It was a win, win, win situation. The girl has a nice nest egg for the rest of her life, Joe has the largest fee he has ever seen, and Dolly Goff didn't have to go to court. By the way, that case is why we were invited tonight."

"You certain it wasn't a win, win, win, win situation?"

"In what way?"

"Didn't our conniving little counselor get a nice big fee for the firm?" Pam's expression was more of a smirk than a smile.

Rick carefully looked around them. He then brushed his wife's hair back and placed his mouth close to her ear. He thrust his tongue into to her ear.

Pam squealed. "Dammit, will you quit that!"

"Would you two prefer if we found you a nice quiet bedroom?"

Pam was crimson when she turned to face Louise McIntosh, the realtor who had sold them their house. "Louise, how wonderful to see you. You remember my adolescent husband, Rick?"

"Of course. This is my husband, Colonel McIntosh. Dear meet Pam and Rick Wilson. They bought one of my listings in Springfield a few months ago."

The two women made small talk while the men looked bored. Finally the Colonel said, "If you good people will excuse me, I need to find where Goff keeps his good stuff. Miz Wilson, it's been my pleasure. Rick, hope to see you again. Maybe we can have lunch sometime." He left.

"I hate to sound like a parrot, but there's Mike Dean from the firm. I need to touch base with him. Excuse me please." Rick was gone too.

"Men just cannot handle shopping or cocktail parties. Tell me, what do you think of Dolly?"

Pam mulled over a response for several seconds. That was some loaded question. Phony, insincere, air-head, bottle blond? "She's just as sweet and friendly as I've heard."

"Oh yes. She plays her role well. I've handled some of her real estate dealings. She can drive you to distraction. She wanted to buy this office complex over in Bethesda and I got her a great price with a thirty-day option. They wanted five hundred thousand in cash up front though. Well. She couldn't raise it, and couldn't raise it, I thought for sure we had lost the deal. Then the day before the option expired, she called me. I came next door here and out of the blue she handed me two checks for two hundred-fifty thousand each."

"Congratulations. That sounds like a nice sale."

"Darling, when the tax people got through, I didn't even have enough left to buy a decent Armani. What do you think of the Colonel? Isn't he an absolute dear?"

"He seems so charming, a real southern gentleman. You rarely see them - -"

"Niles, Niles Carter, you come over here right this second!"

Louise waved her hand in the air as she looked over Pam's shoulder. Pam turned to face a slightly-built man she would classify as dapper. Wavy silver hair, a broad smile, very expensive charcoal gray suit, shirt open at the collar, a silk scarf, all sitting on black and white Italian shoes. Niles Carter carried himself with extreme cockiness.

"Louise it's so good to see you here tonight. How are you my precious love?"

"Wonderful. Don't you just adore the Goff's parties?"

"Yeah, sure."

"Niles I want you to meet one of my special clients, Pam Wilson. They bought in Springfield."

"That's an adequate area. How do you like living in DC?" Niles' eyes darted around the room as he talked.

"Oh darling, they have lived here forever. Mount Vernon, Georgetown, Dale City, now Springfield. Her husband is with the O'Dell firm. You know, you may have known Pam's father. He lived in DC and spent a number of years in Asia."

"Dear Louise thinks that all the senior people in State know everyone and everything. Not that she isn't correct, of course." Niles paused for his importance to sink in. "What's his name?"

"Anders, Bill Anders. He was a retired Army Colonel."

For a flicker of a second Niles' smile froze and a look of fear filled his eyes. He quickly recovered his composure. "No, I didn't know him. Well, I must run." Niles turned and walked away.

Pam thought his actions weird, but Louise didn't seem to notice Niles' abrupt departure. "I think we were talking about the Colonel?" Pam ventured.

"Oh yes. Old Kentucky family. Old Kentucky whiskey family. I'm his second wife. When we married, he was overweight and did precious more than drink all day. I got him to lose some weight, start playing golf regularly, and to even stop drinking before lunch. At least, most of the time. I must say I have been a wonderful influence on him."

Pam wondered if Louise would ever quit talking.

"Also, I'm the one who directed him into politics. Not as a politician, of course, but giving money to the right candidates. The Colonel's a major supporter of our Prentiss Puckett, one of the most senior senators in Washington you know. I haven't seen him yet, but he's supposed to be here tonight."

Pam considered falling down and pretending to be dead if it would get this woman to stop jabbering and leave.

"We're always invited to these parties. The Colonel's also a heavy giver to the party. Well darling, I must run. If I don't get at least a million dollars in listings tonight, I'll be devastated. We'll visit more later."

Pam was left standing alone which she hated. Maybe a hundred people milling around and here's Pam looking like a mousey brunette wallflower. Pam smiled at her humor. On the far wall she spotted a three foot tall ice sculpture of an elephant. Ice sculptures meant food. She walked in that direction. After a few steps a hand roughly grabbed her shoulder from behind. She spun around prepared to tear into somebody.

CHAPTER 11
DUTCH

*P*am exclaimed, "Dutch! I am so glad to see you!" They embraced and Pam kissed the older man on his mouth.

"A kiss like that will get you anything." They faced each other holding hands. "It's been a while."

"Years."

Pam studied the older man. He was not as big as her father and he had the look of an aging athlete, twenty pounds or so of excess weight. His blond hair and blue eyes spoke of a northern European. On closer look Pam saw the puffy face and watery eyes. Dutch's life style was catching up with him. *Still, in his day I'll bet he had his pick of good-looking women.*

"Yes it has. We need to catch up on old times. Where's your hubby Rick?"

"Playing lawyer. If you plan to visit with me, you'll have to feed me, I'm starving."

"Nobody ever starves at a Trevor Goff party. This way, my dear."

Dutch placed one hand around Pam's waist and waved to a waiter with his other. He propelled her toward the frozen elephant. After a dozen boiled shrimp and unnumbered crackers covered with imported caviar, Pam announced she would probably live. As they left the table, Pam grabbed Dutch's arm.

"See that man standing by himself over there? The one with the pink tinted glasses."

"Uh-huh, I don't think I know him. Shouldn't we find Rick? I wouldn't want him to think I've stolen you."

"I'm certain that man was at the funeral and a few weeks ago I saw him on CNN testifying before congress. Rick checked it out and told me he's some big shot with the CIA. When Daddy went to Thailand, I'm certain he worked closely with the CIA. That man must have known my father. I just want to say hello to him."

Pam walked toward him with Dutch at her heels, her attention directed to a medium height, muscular man with close cropped brown hair, a stony face, and those glasses.

The man watched them approach.

"Hello Dutch."

Pam was speechless.

"Hi Mark. I'd like you to meet a friend of mine. Pam Wilson, Mark Harris." Harris looked at her with a complete lack of expression and total indifference.

"Hello. I hate to bother you but I'm certain you knew my late parents and I just wanted to speak to you."

Another man walked past them. "Hey Cobra, how's it going?"

Harris glared at the speaker. "Who were your parents?"

"Bill and Betty Anders, they - -"

"I'm sorry Mrs. . . . ah . . . ah . . . Wilson, but I have no idea who you're talking about. If you will excuse me, I have important things I must do. Good evening Dutch. I'll see you later." Mark Harris turned and left.

Pam was stunned. Harris was the second person to walk away from her that evening with the mention of her parents' names. Pam turned facing Dutch.

"I thought you said you didn't know him? He certainly seemed to recognize you."

"I know him. He's a jerk. I figured he'd be rude or something like that. He does that all the time. I didn't want you embarrassed or your feelings hurt."

"I'm curious, why did that man call Mr. Harris, Cobra?"

"That was his CIA code name once. I guess he liked it since he still uses it."

"One more question Dutch, why does he wear those strange pink tinted glasses?"

"He told me once something happened to his eyes as a kid. Frankly, I think he wears them to look sinister. There's Rick. He's coming this way."

"Hi Dutch."

"Hi yourself." The men shook hands.

"I've missed you, what ya' been doing?" Pam asked.

"Talking about the merger and how bad the Redskins will be this year. Did Dutch feed you?"

"Yes, and he saw to it that I didn't stand around with an empty glass in my hand all night."

"Ouch."

"Actually Rick, Dutch and I are catching up on the last few years so if you need more time."

"Thank you, honey, I really do."

Dutch slipped his arm around Pam's waist again. "No sooner said than done. Let me show you the garden. It's copied after a temple garden in Kyoto, Japan. It's so beautiful the Goff's should really charge admission just to look at it."

Dutch had not exaggerated. They toured the softly lighted grounds passing by miniature stone lanterns, clumps of lotus plants, and down a winding path under a canopy of intertwined vines. They sat down inside an oriental-style gazebo.

"It's so peaceful out here." Pam inhaled a deep breath. "What is that? It smells heavenly."

Dutch chuckled. "Probably some exotic oriental plant Dolly Goff paid too much for."

"This place is gorgeous. With two brownstones and this garden the Goffs must have a fortune tied up here."

"Don't quote me, but I've heard it's well over four million."

"And I thought we paid too much for our place."

"You lived down in Dale City didn't you? Did you move?"

"Yes. The higher Rick gets in the firm the more hours he has to work and that commute back and forth was killing him. I finally brought myself to sell the folks' house. That and the profit on our old place got us into Springfield. We moved a few months ago."

"I feel for you. I moved about six months ago, but I had an easy move. A bachelor only has so much and I still haven't unpacked all my stuff."

"Where's your new place?" A waiter appeared with another drink. "This has got to be my last one. I'm really starting to feel these now."

"Don't worry you're in good hands. My place? You know those condos just south of Old Town, right on the Potomac?"

"Uh-huh." Pam had seen them advertised in the paper and knew they cost more than a million dollars. "Are you still with the same law firm?"

Obviously Dutch did better as a lawyer than Rick or Bill Anders. Her father said Dutch acted as though he had only one client, the trust company next to his office. When you had one client that paid that well, why fool with a big practice. She must remember to tell Rick that.

"Yeah. I'm too lazy to look for anything better. I understand you're nosing around about what happened to your folks?"

"Yes, a little bit. That article by Ned Breaker about them in *The Review* got me started."

"Pam let me give you some excellent advice. Be careful digging into something like this. You may not like what you find. It may not be at all what you think. You understand me?"

Pam ignored the implied question.

Dutch continued talking. "I guess it was rough selling your folks' old place after what happened there?"

"Yes it was." The visions of her mother and father lying on the floor swam before her eyes.

"It must have been horrible for Betty. Hearing that first shot go whizzing past her head knowing the next one she wouldn't hear, 'cause that's the one that would get her. My first tour in Vietnam, I heard a shot go over my head. Fortunately the next one missed too. Your mom wasn't so lucky."

Tears cascaded down Pam's cheeks and splashed on the front of her dress. She wished Dutch would shut his damn mouth.

"I'm sorry. May I borrow your handkerchief please?"

Dutch handed her the folded white square. She held it to her face. "Dutch, please - - "

"I can't imagine how terrible it was for you to walk in there and see them gunned down like helpless animals."

"I need to go back inside."

Pam put her half empty glass on a table and headed into the brownstone. Dutch walked a step behind her.

Rick was smiling as he walked toward the back of the house. He needed to find Pam, spend some time with her then head for home. He knew she wanted to show off that dress. When he saw her, his smile faded.

"What the hell's going on!"

Dutch started to speak but Pam stopped him. "We were

talking about Mom and Dad and I broke up. I'm sorry. Rick, can we please go home now?"

Pam gave Dutch a cursory hug and walked away. As they left the brownstone, the Marines again came to attention.

***

"Are you asleep?" Rick asked.

"No."

"Do you feel like telling me what happened in the garden with you and Dutch?"

Streetlights and the headlights from passing cars caused flashes of brightness inside their car.

"Dutch talked about my folks and how they were killed and it got to me. He was horrible."

"Why would he do that?"

"I don't know. I thought at first he had too much to drink. But I'm not sure. I'm also not sure how close Dutch and my father really ever were."

"Your dad told me they roomed together and played football together. They worked in the same law firm for a while."

"I know. This is only what Daddy has said. They started their senior year with neither having a roommate. They didn't really pick each other out. The head coach assigned them to the same room. Daddy also said Dutch played just enough football to keep his scholarship. At the law firm I remember Daddy saying something about Dutch spending most of his time fooling with a trust company next to his office. I talked to Dutch more tonight than before in my whole life."

"You seemed so glad to see him."

"I know, like someone coming out of the past. I'll give him the benefit of having had too much to drink. Can I put my head on your shoulder?"

"Of course."

"Good night sweetheart."

"Good night, baby."

Rick looked at his wife and kissed her forehead.

As she drifted to sleep, one thought stuck in her mind, *How did Dutch know I've been looking into what happened to my folks?*

CHAPTER 12
BREAK IN

"**P**am, sorry I'm so late. I know you could just kill me." Lindsey bounded through the front door of her shop. "Everywhere I went there were lines, the traffic's horrid, and two simple things at the bank, they botched up both of them. Can you believe it! It's after four o'clock, is Ricky all right?"

Lindsey Sims was tall and willowy. Her brown hair reached to her shoulders. An oval face was highlighted by two very brown eyes, photogenic cheek bones, and sensual mouth that mirrored every mood. Lindsey's high school yearbook had labeled her vivacious. A very apt description.

The Book Place reflected Lindsey. Shelves of brightly covered books, and an aroma of potpourri made the first impression. A far corner contained a kindergarten size table and chairs. Several soft leather chairs urged patrons to pause and browse.

Pam always thought Lindsey lived faster than time and knew that when Lindsey died she would say something like "sorry to be late for my funeral, traffic was so unreal."

"No problem at all," Pam replied. "On Tuesday and

Thursday Ricky goes straight to his friend Adam's house. I called a while ago and he's fine."

Pam was at work in Lindsey's Book Place. The women had become friends while in Georgetown. When Pam moved from Dale City to within two miles of the store, she was more than happy to work part-time. Having mad money that did not come out of the household budget was nice. She liked getting out with people, loved books, and most of all, thoroughly enjoyed Lindsey's company.

The women chatted. Could Pam come in a few hours on Saturday for a book signing? Of course. After several minutes Pam looked at her watch. "I must get going. I've got errands to run and a dinner to get started."

Pam stopped at a drug store and the cleaners on her way home. After pulling her car into the garage, she walked to their mailbox.

"Hello Pam, how are you?" The speaker was Mr. Cranston, her next door neighbor, now busy watering the plants by his mailbox. Recently retired, he spent most of his time puttering with his flowers or sitting on his porch watching the neighborhood drift by.

Pam waved.

"Hope they got your telephone fixed," Cranston added.

"I'm sorry, what do you mean?" Pam turned and walked toward him.

"The telephone company repair truck came here right after you went out this morning and they only left a few minutes ago. Must have been some real problem I'd reckon. How are your azaleas doing? You need some more of that plant food? I've still got extra."

Pam's brow furrowed. "No. No thanks. Everything's doing fine. If I need any help, I'll holler."

Pam left the house about ten. It was now after four thirty, six and a half hours. No way.

"You sure about the phone company truck?" she asked.

"Positive. I was sitting on the porch when you left, couldn't have gone two blocks when they pulled in. Should say he. Only saw one person. He left the truck down close to the street so I could see it from my place. I was here watering the flowers when he left, and then you pulled in. Yep, I'm sure certain about that truck."

"Thank you, Mr. Cranston. Bye now."

***

Pam walked back to her house, through the garage and into the kitchen. She put the junk mail in the trash, laid her purse on the kitchen table, and continued to the dining room. She put the other mail on the dining room table for Rick when he got home. Then she noticed an envelope on one end of the table and a folded sheet of paper on the other. The envelope had Ricky's teacher's name on it, in her handwriting. She opened the sheet of paper. Across the top was printed, PERMISSION SLIP.

With a gasp Pam slowly looked around. A deadly stillness filled the house. The kitchen clock's ticking sounded like a deathwatch beetle. Pam backed into the kitchen, picked up her purse, and left the house through the garage's rear door. She crossed two back yards, using the newly installed gate, to reach Gabby's house.

"Come on in, the door's unlocked. I can tell you Ricky's not ready to leave yet. He's beating Adam about two out of three on Adam's new video game."

Gabby turned to face her friend. "Pam, what in the world's wrong? Is Rick all right?"

Pam reiterated her conversation with Mr. Cranston. She continued, "Ricky was running late for the bus today and forgot the permission slip for their field trip Friday. I put the slip in an envelope with his teacher's name on it and left it on the edge of the dining table. When I got home, the

slip was out of the envelope at one end of the table and the
envelope on the other end."

"You're certain about where you left it?"

"Yes, absolutely."

"Then someone must have been in your house. We've
got to call the cops."

"I can't do that."

"Why not!"

"Look. I lied to Rick about Breaker. Told him we went
to Breaker's office. The shit's going to hit the fan if the
truth ever comes out. We were on the verge of a real knock
down drag out argument over Morris. And I lied to Rick
about going to see Khan. I said I went to New York to do
some stuff for Lindsey. If the police come and question me,
some or all of this has got to come out. We'll end up in a
Breaker column as the Omaha hookers, screw up our
husbands' careers, and to top it all off Rick will probably
kick my butt out of the house."

"My friend, the little black cloud. I do see what you
mean though. Let's think this through. Who could have
been in your house? First, Ricky came straight here. What
about Rick? Could he have run home for something?"

"No, it's a good thirty five minutes each way. Anyway
he called about two or so at Lindsey's. If he had any plans
to come to the house, he would have said something."

"Okay. Call the phone company and see if they had
repair work at your house today. While you do that I'll get
my things together."

Gabby put dinner on hold, checked on the boys, and
went into her bedroom. When she returned to the kitchen,
Pam looked even grimmer.

"I guess I know the answer, huh?"

Pam nodded.

"I was afraid of this. Let's go kid."

"Why do you have Brad's handgun in your waistband?"

"It's not Brad's, it's mine."

"Gabby answer my question."

"You told me Cranston said the truck came and went in perfect timing with your departure and arrival back home, right?"

"Yes."

"That means someone was watching you. That also means someone knew you were alone. You walk in the house, someone cuts your throat, the truck picks that person up, and they find the truck a week from now in a parking lot two counties away."

Pam's voice sounded feeble. "Mr. Cranston said there was only one person in the truck and why would somebody want to kill me?"

"Cranston only saw one person. And, why did somebody want to kill your parents?"

"Let's go. Do you need that?" Pam pointed to Gabby's waist.

"Yes, it's better to have your piece a thousand times and not need it, than to need it once and not have it."

***

The women searched the house to no avail. They ended in the master bedroom.

"You look in the closets and I'll check the bathroom."

Pam entered her walk-in closet, looked around, and screamed. "Gabby, come here, hurry!"

"What is it?"

"See that red and black shoe box?"

Gabby looked at the more than three dozen shoe boxes on a shelf. "Yeah. What about it?"

"That's a pair of brown snake skin pumps. They're out of style, but I love them, and they cost so much I can't bring myself to get rid of them."

"I understand that. So?"

"Since I never wear them, I keep them on the upper right side of that shelf out of the way. Look where they are now."

Gabby looked, the red and black shoe box was on the far left side of the bottom shelf.

***

The two women sat at Pam's kitchen table. After several minutes of silence, Gabby spoke. "I guess we could say somebody went through your house all right."

"Who and why?"

"No idea." Maybe you've irritated somebody by checking on that Breaker story. What I do know is at this point you need some professional help."

"Gabby, I went through that with Rick. Right after the folks were murdered, I went to two different shrinks. Neither one of 'em did me any good."

"No, what I mean is a private investigator or detective, something like that."

"I'd have no idea who to call."

"I know of someone. I've got to check with Brad to make sure it's okay. I'll call you as soon as I can." Gabby stood up to leave. "Will you be all right alone?"

"Hey I'm great. I didn't get my throat cut yet and none of our valuables were taken. When I was a kid, I read an Edgar Rice Burroughs book about Mars. The hero John Carter, when he would get in a jam, would say, 'I'm not dead yet.' That's kind of how I feel now."

Gabby laughed out loud. "You're absolutely too much. If I set out to create a crazy friend, I'd use you as the model."

Pam flushed. "Thank you." She looked into her friend's dark brown eyes. "Gabby, what kind of Pandora's box have I opened?"

"I wish I knew."

CHAPTER 13
MALONE

P am stood in the hall of an Arlington office building. On a frosted glass panel in the door, a sign read:

FRANK MALONE
Private Investigator

Not at all like New York. Pam took a deep breath and opened the door. A secretary looked up from her work. "Mrs. Wilson?"

"Yes."

"Mr. Malone's expecting you. Have a seat, he'll be with you in a second. Care for some coffee, soft drink?"

"No thank you." Pam sat in a leather side chair and took the office in with one swift glance. Two groups of two chairs like this one, end tables in between, lamps, magazines, and office type art on the walls. A door facing the hall was closed. Another door stood half open and revealed file cabinets. In Pam's mind it looked like a set for a Sam Spade movie, only nicer. According to the nameplate on her desk, the secretary was Patsy. Very blond, very made up, very sexy, and judging from the speed with which she typed on a PC from handwritten notes, very competent.

Yesterday afternoon, twenty minutes after she left Pam's house, Gabby phoned. She had talked to Brad and the detective. Pam should call the detective before he goes home. A thirty minute conversation with Frank Malone led to a two o'clock appointment this afternoon.

Pam waited for the door to open and Bogey walk out. The door opened, but it wasn't Bogart. Frank Malone stood six feet two maybe, two hundred pounds plus, thinning red hair, a ruddy face, and a little boy smile. All he needed was a green necktie that said, "Kiss me, I'm Irish."

"Mrs. Wilson, Pamela, Pam? Which do you prefer?"

"Pam, please. You're Mr. Malone?"

The Irishman smiled. "Frank, please."

Malone escorted Pam into his office which looked even more like a movie set. A desk and executive chair, side chairs by the desk, an oval conference table piled with a manila folder and pads of paper, mandatory bookcases, and more office prints. A diploma from Villanova and several citations hung on the wall behind Malone's desk. Even from half way across the room Pam could see J. Edgar Hoover's signature on one of the awards.

Malone directed Pam toward the table. She selected a chair facing him.

"So you're a friend of the Petersens?"

"We're neighbors. Gabby said you and Brad used to work together?"

"I wouldn't put it quite like that. We worked on cases together. I retired from the IRS with twenty-four years in fraud. Several times I worked with Brad and the FBI. Since I retired and opened this shop, I'm doing a fair amount of contract work for the Bureau. Brad seems to find a lot of things for me to handle."

Pam wondered what he was talking about, but decided she probably shouldn't ask. "I'm really glad you could work me into your schedule. I think I need help."

Another teddy bear smile as Malone sat down. "Hey it's my pleasure. I owe Brad several favors, and like I always say, given a choice, I'd always rather represent a pretty damsel in distress than most anything."

Pam blushed, but she felt comfortable with the calm, low-key Frank Malone.

Malone picked up a piece of paper. "From our discussion yesterday, I've formed five questions you need answered, if we can. Who is Steve Morris, who is Rajah Khan, what happened in New York, who went through your house, and who killed your parents?"

Pam pursed her lips and pestered a lock of hair. "I don't think I mentioned that last one did I?"

"No, you didn't."

"You know, Frank, that's really what this has come to. I mean, it began with me wanting to find out why Ned Breaker wrote that article and where he got his information. Well, now I think I've found that out. But actually I don't know any more than when I started. I've always thought my folks were just in the wrong place at the wrong time. Now I'm not sure what happened to them. Does that make any sense to you?"

"It makes perfectly good sense to me. Ready?"

"Yes, should I take notes?"

"Wouldn't hurt." Malone pushed a pad and pencil to her. "Interrupt me any time, okay?"

Pam picked up the pencil.

"Morris. He shows up in Vietnam working for the Pacific Architects and Engineers, P A and E, civilian contractors." Malone looked at Pam and smiled.

Pam smiled back and thought he must mean that's not really what they were.

"Morris also did work for the CIA, AID, South Vietnamese, and probably the VC. Anything for a buck. After the war he drifted around the area. Singapore, Jakarta, Manila, a professional expatriate, ending up in Bangkok. You know the rest from there?"

"I think so."

"Global and Morris have filed all of their tax returns on time and paid all of their taxes. That's a big thing to Revenue Agents. Now, Rajah Khan. I must say lady you pick some very weird playmates."

Pam sat upright. "Hey, wait a minute Frank, I've never even seen the guy."

"That's probably a lucky break for you. Even though Khan's well into his seventies now, I don't think he would be a good one to mess with."

And Pam believed she was going to have lunch with the man and exchange idle chit chat.

"After the second war, he shows up as a big player in white slavery. Moves into extortion, drugs, and finally, what becomes his first love, money laundering. Very active in Vietnam. But I found nothing linking him with the story Morris told you about losing five million. The last Vietnam MPC conversion had some irregularities, the South Koreans possibly, but definitely some US Government agencies. CIA, AID, State maybe. One thing, after that last conversion, diplomatic notes were exchanged between Seoul and Washington. One report called them scathing, but they were both ignored. Now it's going to start getting complicated. If you get lost let me know. I'll try to just stay with the high points."

"So far so good. Carry on."

"Fifteen or so years ago drugs and money laundering were out of control worldwide. It had reached the point where in some places, bad money overwhelmed good money, economies and monetary systems had collapsed.

The Pacific Rim, Central and South America in particular. There was fear that more than one hundred billion in loans would be defaulted to places such as Bank of America and Barclays. This with no prayer of them ever being repaid. The financial world would have gone to hell."

Malone paused and looked through his notes. "I put this together after we talked yesterday. I want to make certain I haven't left out anything important."

"How did you get all of this together so quick?"

"You have to know where to look. Okay, here we are. The big drug money, hundreds of billions a year, is handled by the cartels and mafia. Left over are hundreds of millions, too small to fool with, or too hard. This is the world Khan and his type worked. Small potatoes, but still a whole lot of money there. When things had really gotten bad, the big banks, World Bank, IMF, FBI, Interpole, Moussad, among others, got together and slammed the lid shut. The big guys had the resources and clout to weather the storm. The little players were dying. Somehow Khan got through it. By now he had a major operation in North America with headquarters in lower Manhattan, the place where you went."

"It's a dinky little hole in the wall."

"When you went there it was. Before Lee got busted and ratted on Khan, they had all of one floor and parts of two others. Somehow Swiss Trading got a thirty-year lease for seven to eight dollars a square foot. Probably coercion. When Khan had to start shutting down his North American operation thanks to Bill Lee, he just sublet that space for thirty-five dollars a foot or more. Phillip manages the rentals and keeps a place for Khan's folks to hang their hat when they're in town."

"Where's Khan now?"

"He has a villa outside Berne. Probably there, but he really hasn't surfaced anywhere for a good five years."

"Is he still alive? Pam asked.

Malone shrugged his shoulders.

She continued, "What about New York?"

"Pam, do you realize there are probably only this many Caucasian women in the world who know the stuff you told Phillip?" Malone held his hand facing Pam with his thumb bent down.

"I guess I didn't."

"After you called, Phillip got on the horn with somebody, somewhere. You must have scared the living crap out of 'em. A ghost from the past, or what? I believe they brought you to New York just to find out who you were and what you wanted. You said Phillip gave you a glossy print to look at?"

"Yes, I suspected a trap, but it was just a bunch of girls and two guys in front of a building. I looked it over like I cared and handed it back to Phillip."

"And Phillip took it carefully by a corner and left for about twenty minutes?" Malone asked.

"Yes. Maybe a little longer. He was gone when I saw the movement inside the mirror."

Malone held up his hand. "Not quite so fast. When you handled the picture, you left some fine fingerprints. Phillip most likely ran you through AFIAS."

"What's that?"

"Stands for Automated Fingerprint Identification and Authentication System. It's a database of virtually everyone who has ever been fingerprinted. You pay a fee for access and need some special equipment. In Khan's business, I'm sure he would have had it. If you're not online, it takes fifteen plus minutes to run. Have you ever worked for the government?"

"I worked at Justice for about six years after I got out of collage."

"You're in there then. The mirror's two way, Phillip

watched you and probably took some pictures, more identification. He got careless and opened a door or something with a light on. That's what you saw. When they decided you were not from an enemy camp, an international assassin, or a Government agent, they lost interest in you."

"That brings us to who broke into my house. From what you're saying Phillip did not come down from New York and do it." Pam looked at her pad. It contained a series of concentric circles. She laid the pencil down. As thorough as Malone was, she had found nothing to write.

"For now I would say no. I talked to your Mr. Cranston. He didn't ask and I didn't say if I'm a cop. He thought I was and told me everything he told you plus some."

"Plus what?"

"He described the truck to me. It wasn't a phone company truck, just made to look like one. Something a big-time operation would have. The timing was just as close as you thought. Somebody had you in sight all day. It wouldn't do for you to come home while they were there. Cranston said he only saw one, maybe he's right. If so, the guy's an even bigger pro than I would have thought."

"Frank, I'm sorry, you're losing me."

"You told me your normal schedule. They could figure on only four hours to go through your house. They lucked out and got six. Then they left a few signs to let you know they were there. There are probably some others you missed."

"All right, what were they looking for?"

"I have no earthly idea, nor do I have any idea why they left signs for you to find."

"And we don't know who murdered my folks either do we?"

"No. If it's Khan, he's settling a thirty-year-old score. Highly unlikely. If not Khan, then who?"

Pam slumped in her chair. "What you're saying is that we've hit a dead end. I mean, we have nothing at all to go on, do we?"

"Oh Lord no, we're just getting started." Malone beamed as he leaned back in his chair. "You told me you're available tomorrow. We're set to go through the Mount Vernon police files in the morning. Sunshine laws you know. Then we'll go from there."

"What are we looking for in the police files? What could we possibly find that someone didn't see fourteen months ago?"

"You said a few minutes ago that you don't know anymore now than when you began. That's technically true I guess. But stop and realize how much more you know today about what may have led to your parents' death than anyone could have imagined fourteen months ago. Then it was, for all intents and purposes, a random act of violence. No reason to expect anything more.

"I know Ned Breaker, his guess as to what happened to them was nothing more than a guess. For once he may have been right. I can't say that it was premeditated murder, but I have a strong feeling that your parents were killed by someone who intentionally meant to do them harm. Viewed from that light, things might look important today that may not have looked important fourteen months ago."

"I understand what you're saying. When you look at it that way it gets exciting as opposed to depressing."

"Speaking of depressing. Tomorrow you're my client. That means that legally you have to give me a retainer. That okay?"

"Of course, how much?"

"Let's see, I do owe Brad, and he did send an attractive client for a change. Oh, how about fifty dollars?"

"Are you serious?"

Another Malone smile. "I can make it more if you want

me to. Certainly don't want you to think you got a cut rate private eye."

"No. That's fine. I'll write you a check."

While Pam took care of the check, Malone said, "Does tomorrow here at nine work for you? We can go over there in my car."

"That's fine." Pam stood up. "I'll see you in the morning."

"Have a good evening."

"I will Frank, you too."

Pam walked through the outer office past Malone's secretary and into the hall. "Good bye Patsy."

Patsy looked up from her desk, "Bye now, Mrs. Wilson."

***

Frank Malone walked to his desk. For several minutes he sat in thought.

Patsy's intercom flashed. "Yes sir."

"Uh . . . Patsy . . . get an envelope and write Pam Wilson's name on it. Please come in and get her check, put it in the envelope, and lock it in our safe. You finished with that other report?"

"Yes sir."

"Bring it in when you come."

CHAPTER 14
POLICE STATION

Breakfast was finished." Looks like we'll finalize plans for the merger trip to San Francisco today," Rick commented over the last of his coffee.

"Are you still going to head up your group for the negotiations?" Pam asked.

"I think so. Mr. Goldman will come out toward the end of the week to review everything, and I'll touch base with the office every day, but basically I've got the ball."

Pam tapped her chin. "Where have I heard his name lately?"

"He was in on the Goff lawsuit I told you about. Believe it or not he had never done a personal liability suit before and he thought it was a hoot. He's the senior partner on the merger and we work great together."

"I wish I could get some pom-poms and lead cheers for you."

"Wouldn't that be a riot? Right in the middle of an overly serious deliberation have a bunch of cheerleaders burst in and start leading cheers for the plaintiff."

"Has anyone ever told you that you're a very weird lawyer?"

They both laughed.

"Looks like the team will leave Sunday and we'll kick it off Monday morning. It should take all week. What's on your agenda for today?"

Pam thought for a second. *Why do I have to keep lying to him.*

"I need to do some shopping and run errands. A woman's never too busy to look for shoes."

Rick smiled at her humor. "I love you so much Pam. You have stopped chasing after that bunch that talked to Breaker haven't you? I'd hate for you to be the next victim."

***

Frank Malone nosed his car into a space marked visitors only. As they walked into the building, he warned Pam, "You're going to see that police work's at least ninety percent paper and reports. Let's both go through each file, that way we're less apt to miss something."

Pam had no idea what to look for in the files.

The Mount Vernon Police Department consisted of a white one-story building, built originally in the seventies, but added to twice.

Pam noted in spite of its age, the paint was fresh and the small grassy areas and shrubs neatly manicured.

Inside, Malone spoke to a uniformed officer behind a desk that dominated the entrance. In a few minutes another officer appeared. "You Mr. Malone?"

"Yes. This is my client, Mrs. Wilson."

The officer led them through a door into the heart of the station house. They walked down a hall, turned left past a door marked "Files and Records - Authorized Personnel

Only" to a plain metal door. She looked at Malone, "You've done this before?"

Malone nodded.

"You can't bring anything in so you'll need a locker for your purse and briefcase. This way."

That taken care of, they entered the unmarked room. One four by five foot metal table and a half a dozen metal chairs comprised the furniture. On the table sat two five-inch stacks of file folders, lined pads, pencils and red paper clips. The officer droned her canned instructions. "Nothing comes out of a file and nothing goes into a file. Do not write in a file. Keep your hands in full view at all times. Failure to follow these rules is a misdemeanor punishable by up to thirty days in jail and a fine not to exceed twenty-five hundred dollars. Do you both understand?" They nodded. She looked at Malone. "You know how to use the clips to request copies?" Another nod. "Good. I'll be sitting over there. About how long you think you'll take?"

"Easy three hours, maybe more."

"You want me to get some sandwiches for you when we call in our lunch order?"

"No thanks, we'll grab something later."

Malone pushed one stack in front of Pam. "You start with these. When you finish one put it here. I'll put mine here. Ready?"

"Ready."

***

Pam stood up, checked her watch, one thirty. She looked at Malone. *My tail's petrified from that metal chair and if we don't eat soon, I'll faint. Frank, tell the lady we'll pick our copies up later. Let's go.*

"We'll just wait out front for the copies, if that's all right." Malone had missed Pam's unspoken plea.

"Sure, looks like only a dozen or so, maybe fifteen minutes."

Finally they left the police station.

"You hungry?" Malone asked.

"Starving."

"There's a great deli down the street. Want to stop?"

"You mean Dino's?"

"Yeah, how'd you know?"

"I grew up here."

"Oh."

***

Dino's looked just like Pam remembered. Maroon and chrome furniture stood on black and white tile squares. A pungent odor of garlic filled the air. By two o'clock it was nearly empty and no music came from the multi-colored juke box on the back wall. They placed their orders and Malone looked at Pam.

"You go first. Anything worth pursuing?"

"I don't know. I couldn't look at the pictures of my parents. In fact I'm surprised I could even go through those files. Two months ago I would have taken one look at them and bawled."

"I think you'll find the more active you get in your pursuit of answers the easier it'll be."

"I hope you're right. The only thing I did notice was the extent to which those jerks trashed the house. I don't remember that morning and after the police finally left, Mother's friends pretty much put it back together. The police shot pictures of everything. Drawers pulled out, then turned upside down with everything dumped out and furniture turned over. Daddy had a small wooden file cabinet that Mom gave him. They turned that upside down and pulled the drawers out."

Malone thought for a long minute. "Pam, if you're trying to find a basketball, where would you look?"

"I don't know, a gym maybe?"

"Sorry. Bad question. Where would you look for something shaped like a basketball?"

"Oh, I see what you mean. Probably in some place big enough to hold a basketball."

"I studied those pictures and you've come to the same conclusion I did."

"What conclusion? I still don't get what we're talking about."

"Whoever tore up the house searched for something flat. Something you could hide by taping on a drawer bottom, under a chair, something like that. What in hell could that be?"

"Frank, I have no idea. Hopefully you came up with a lot more than I did."

"I've got a few things." He shifted through several pieces of paper. "Did you know your father had a Rolls Royce computer?"

"Rick told me he spent a lot of money on it and it was better than what they have in Rick's law offices. Mom said Daddy would spend hours working on it. Always at night and on weekends."

"When did that start?"

"Eight or nine months before they were murdered, I think."

"Your dad had twelve secure files in his computer that he erased. An expert the local police called in from the Commonwealth police broke the security, but when he got into them all the data was gone. What do you make of that? As much as it appears your dad knew about computers he must have realized that no matter how much security he put into place, the data could be retrieved. So he erased the files several times and put the information somewhere else.

Where, I have no idea."

Their lunch arrived. Pam took a bite of pastrami and Swiss on rye, Dino's specialty. She felt she should add something to this, but had no idea what.

"He also hacked into the bank's files. Not hard to do and as he was a vice president, maybe not unusual. Since it is a bank, the police referred this to Treasury for advice on how to proceed. In three days they got an answer from an Assistant Secretary of the Treasury directing the police not to pursue the matter as Treasury had already investigated it. How does that strike you?"

Pam had discovered Frank did not always expect an answer to his questions. She ate in silence.

Malone continued. "This is a jerkwater little bank. I can't conceive of an assistant secretary getting involved. Some crazy damn place."

"What came out of it?"

"According to the police files nothing. Next item. A man who lived across the street from your folks took his dog for a walk at nine thirty-five that night."

Pam studied her sandwich. "Wait a minute. How did he know the exact time?"

"His favorite TV show ended, he peed, got his dog on a leash and went out."

Pam blushed and attacked her sandwich again.

"He saw a car in your folk's driveway. The man and dog went around the block and got back to the house about twenty minutes later and the car was still there."

"Great, did he get the license number?"

"No, he didn't even think about it. He said it looked like a big American make, gold or light brown. What'd your folks have?"

"A white Buick."

"Nothing there for now. Your folks had caller ID, their last fifty calls are here." Malone handed some papers to

Pam. "This list has calls on their answering machine." He handed Pam another piece of paper. "Your father took his last call at 9:08 that night, same person who called him several times on Thursday and Friday. The first unanswered call on the answering machine came from you at 10:05, almost an hour later."

"Yes, I called to remind Mom that I'd be there in time for us to go to lunch before we went shopping. Then we were all going to eat dinner at the folk's house that evening." Tears began running down Pam's cheeks.

"I'm sorry." Malone gave Pam his handkerchief and waited until she regained her composure.

"You okay now?"

"Yes. Go on."

"The police still have this as unsolved, but they believe some crack-heads killed your folks. That's why, according to them, the place was ransacked. The police put the time of death between midnight and two in the morning. Their logic runs like this. Due to the noise, it happened after the neighbors had gone to bed and were asleep. Also, a clock in the spare bedroom had been unplugged at twelve forty-five."

"What!" Pam's eyes grew wide as she leaned across the table. Iced tea glasses wobbled. "That's the clock I gave Mom when I was pregnant with Ricky. She loved it so much that when it stopped working, she still kept it but moved it to the guest bedroom for a decoration. Frank, that must have been five years ago. She always talked about getting it fixed, but never did."

"Well damnation. You certain about that?"

Pam nodded her head vigorously. "Absolutely."

"Then the clock theory's meaningless. So they could have been murdered between 9:08 and 10:05. I didn't see any other answer, but I couldn't overcome the clock. It's a whole new ball game now. What about your call?"

"I just figured they had gone out, but they couldn't have with a car parked in their driveway. Wait, if they were murdered between nine and ten, then that car might be the killer's."

Malone looked at Pam. "Good thinking. But the killer wouldn't park in your folk's driveway. What we have is one of two things: the person was in the house when the murders took place, or . . ." Malone paused for a moment. ". . . maybe the murders were not premeditated, they just happened. I wish we had some way to identify the car. We don't so we've got to go at it from a different direction. I want you to take these caller ID phone numbers and see who they're from. Also, the numbers from the answering machine. The only thing in the police files is a note that nothing was significant about the calls. We need to start constructing what may have happened on those last two days. Remember, what wasn't significant then might be critical now."

"What are the calls with the phone number shown as seven asterisks?"

"From secure telephones."

"Such as."

"If the President of the United States called you on his red phone, it would record as a series of asterisks."

"You mean like your password on a computer?"

"Uh-huh."

"Can we get the number?"

"Since these phones are part of our national security system, the answer is no."

"What if we could prove they're related to the murders?"

"Maybe, but probably not."

"So we go from here?"

"Yep, we play the cards we're holding and go forward from here."

CHAPTER 15
THE KEY

With her son at a birthday party and her husband on the golf course, Pam enjoyed some Saturday morning solitude. Clad in cut off jeans, a sleeveless tee, and barefoot, she sat at the kitchen table holding an open container of yogurt. Pam often mused that considering how much yogurt she ate, if it wasn't for low fat, she would be as big as a barn. Her eyes surveyed the papers on the table. Caller ID Listing, Answering Machine Transcripts, and To Do. She picked up the latter sheet.

Finish phone calls was checked, Pam's shorthand, meaning she was working on it, but had not finished.

Ricky to party. Pam lined through this item. "Gabby should be back soon from taking the boys."

Pick up Ricky. "I've got to ask Gabby what time they're through."

Book signing, 1-3. "It's almost eleven. I need to start getting ready about twelve or so."

Dinner at Petersen's. Pam thought this was sweet of Gabby. Rick was leaving for California tomorrow and it would be great not to cook tonight. They could come home, put Ricky to bed and scratch the itch Pam had developed. Pam smiled and curled her bare toes around the chair rungs.

"Hi Pam." Gabby came in through the kitchen door. "What's ya eating?"

"Peach yogurt. There's more in the frig if you want some."

Gabby found a container and spoon, and sat down facing Pam.

"What time am I supposed to pick up the boys?"

"Kim said about three-thirty. Can you believe she has twelve little boys ages nine and ten in that house? That's nuts. When it's Adam's turn, it's a fast-food burger and a movie. They can stand in the front yard until their mothers pick 'em up."

"You say that but you don't mean it."

"Just watch. Anyway, how are you coming with those phone calls?"

Pam picked up the answering machine list. "Good and not so good. These were easy. First one was me. Next four were Dad's golfing buddies telling him to hurry up, he was late. Last one came from the yard man calling about Mom's new plants."

"Okay, what about the other list."

Pam now picked up the caller ID sheet. "This covers about two weeks of phone calls. It's funny, phone calls almost define our life. Calls from Mom's friends, the hairdresser, Dad's golfing buddy, some that must have been solicitors, and a couple of men Dad had talked to about moving their accounts to his bank. Just the odds and ends that make up day-to-day living."

"You make it sound boring as heck. I thought you said some of it was not so good."

"There are two numbers I can't do anything with. The asterisk number and another one that called four times on

Thursday and Friday. The secure number could be nothing. Dad spent thirty years in the Army and five years in AID. He knew people all over the government, probably including some in the CIA. A lot of different folks could have called on a phone like that. What makes me wonder though is that those two calls are almost linked to the other mystery number."

Gabby put her container and spoon in the sink and sat back down. "Sorry, Pam I don't follow you."

"On Thursday, about two in the afternoon, mystery number calls, two minutes later, secure phone calls, then a few minutes after that the mystery number calls again. On Friday, mid-afternoon, mystery number, then in minutes, asterisks again." Pam paused and swallowed with difficulty. "Mystery number called again at 9:08, the last call they got before they were murdered."

Gabby eyed Pam and waited. "Sounds like there might be a connection between the two numbers, doesn't it? What's the story on the mystery number?"

"No longer in use. I talked to a supervisor at the phone company but they won't tell me who had it fourteen months or so ago. I worked on this yesterday afternoon and called Malone before he went home. He said the phone company has been burned so many times they will not release that information unless you're the police or have a court order. He doubted at this point we have the basis for a court order."

"That's a hell of a note isn't it. Any other ideas?"

"Yeah. I've got a lot of stuff that Rick took out of Daddy's desk stored up in the attic. I'm going through that and see if anything falls out."

"Well good luck. We'll see you about six?"

"Can I bring anything?"

Gabby shook her head as she left. "See you tonight."

***

Pam gathered the pieces of paper. She was glad she would have something, though not very much, for her Monday meeting with Malone. She put the papers in a dresser drawer and looked at the clock. With thirty minutes before she had to get ready for work, Pam had time to visit the attic. She pulled a cord and the attic stairs came down from the hall ceiling. At the top of the stairs she looked around. Dust on the attic floor was covered in footprints. Pam shivered and an icy pain hit the pit of her stomach. Whoever had gone through her house also searched the attic. Every time she thought about the break-in she felt personally violated.

The attic held Christmas decorations, suitcases, and scattered miscellaneous boxes. Pam found two manila envelopes with her father's things inside. She also found the guest book from the funeral. She could look and see if that weird Mark Harris came; it would be nice to know for sure, assuming he signed the book if he was there.

At the top of the steps, she noticed her mother's jewelry box. She believed now she could go through the jewelry. Betty had some beautiful pieces and Pam knew she would want her daughter to use them. Pam gathered the two envelopes, the guest book, and placed the jewelry case on top. With all this tucked under one arm she began slowly backing down the stairs. After taking two steps the jewelry box slipped from her arm, hit the stairs once, and smashed on the hall floor. Jewelry and pieces of wood flew in all directions.

Pam put the envelopes and guest book on the dining room table. She cried as she went back to the hall and gathered the jewelry. "I'm sorry Mom. You always knew I was a klutz." The jewelry was easy to sort. The pieces of wood were inside dividers. They all slipped into place. It looked like new. She replaced the jewelry planning to sort through it while Rick was in California.

When Pam lifted the box, a piece of wood fell from the bottom. She turned the box over and saw a small compartment under where the wood had been. Wedged inside was a key. Using a table knife she pried the key loose. It looked like nothing she had ever seen. A metal key shaft two inches long with a series of notches on one side. The brass handle was the size of a half dollar, with the numbers 115 stamped on each side.

She stared at the key for several minutes. What had Dutch said? "Be careful digging into something like this, you may not like what you find. It may not be at all what you think." What had Mother kept from Daddy? What was the key for and how long had it been hidden? She studied the box closer. A dowel hidden under velvet inside released the compartment cover. When Pam put the inside partitions back together, she must have pushed on the dowel. Her mind spun. Maybe her father hid the key here and never told Betty. Maybe she had no idea in the world what this was or why it was hidden here. What if they were doing things she never could have imagined? Maybe she would never know? If it was something bad, would she even want to know?

Pam looked at her watch, closed her eyes, and took a deep breath. *I'll worry about this while Rick's gone. Maybe I should show it to Malone? This is going to drive me crazy.*

She hid her father's papers in the hall closet and the key under her lingerie. She had no interest in lying to Rick about the key and where she had found it.

As she showered, Pam remembered that a week ago she planned to have lunch with Rajah Khan and let him explain everything to her. How naive and stupid. Now she had more questions than answers. She spoke aloud to herself.

"I know one thing, Malone is right, the further into this I go, the stronger I get. No more choking up, no more backing off. I don't know who the hell you are or where you are, but Pam Wilson is coming after your damn ass."

CHAPTER 16
AIRPORT

A loud speaker blared above the din of a crowded terminal, "Transnational Flight four fifty-seven from Atlanta now arriving at gate twenty-nine."

Sunday evening at Washington's Reagan National Airport should have been relatively calm. This Sunday was a mad house. A massive storm front had dropped down from Canada and covered an area from Chicago to Cleveland. All flights in the northern United States were grounded. Since Rick's plane came from Chicago, his turnaround flight to San Francisco at five thirty had been delayed. Rick's idea of getting to Reagan early, checking in, and then having a drink in one of the airport lounges was no longer possible. All of the lounges had long since exceeded their legal capacity.

Pam perched on the arm of a waiting area chair. Rick's over filled carry-on leaned against her legs. The digital clock over her head read five ten. Through the crowd she saw Rick elbowing his way toward her. The look on his face answered her question. Bad news. He finally got to her.

"Well?"

"Damn. My plane's still on the ground in Chicago. The storm's breaking up, so it should get off in an hour. But the worst is that they don't expect it here until eight. Maybe."

"Any idea what time you will get in?"

"Doesn't matter too much. I'm first class, so the meal will be good and I'll have plenty of room to sleep. Monday morning's our in-house meeting. If I'm late, it's not that big a deal."

Pam stood up and rubbed her butt. "That's not comfort spot supreme. Do you want to eat now or wait for the airplane meal?"

"Look. You head on home. I'll grab a hot dog or something. There's no need in you hanging around this place. It's like Bedlam on a bad hair day."

Pam laughed. "No way. I can just see it. Tuesday morning they all meet. The Japanese guy says, 'Where's Wilson-san?', somebody else says, 'Oh him, he died on the flight out here from heartburn, he ate an underdone airport hot dog.' And then the Japanese guy stands up and says - -"

Rick laughed. "Hush, you've made your point. You want to get fed." He slid his arm around Pam's waist."

"You always know what to do when I get uptight don't you? Where do you want to go?"

"Remember that place in Old Town, right off Washington, that has the delicious crab cakes? We haven't gone there in ages."

"Sounds good. You get in line for a taxi and I'll go put my stuff in a locker. If we try to take the car we'll never get back in the parking lot."

***

The restaurant had not changed. An aroma of old building and fresh seafood filled the air and clung to the raw brick walls. On Sunday evening it was only half full.

The soft mummer of several unrelated conversations coupled with subdued lighting created an almost dreamlike environment. After dinner, over a second glass of wine, Rick stared at his wife.

"Why are you looking at me like that? I've got a green thing in my front teeth don't I?"

"Pam, you are so beautiful. You have the most fantastic sense of humor I've ever seen. That's one thing that makes you so beautiful. By the way, it's only a little green thing."

"Thank you, sir. You're much too kind. Mother always told me that if I ever found a man I could laugh with as much as she and daddy did to marry him quick before somebody else got him. I think we do pretty well."

Rick smiled and rubbed his wife's hand.

Pam continued. "New subject. Ricky's really excited about going down to your folks this week. You sure they can handle him and Adam both for ten days?"

"You and Gabby always say two of them are easier than one. There's one thing I do want to tell you. I haven't said anything before just in case it doesn't pan out, then there's no need to be disappointed."

"Well, tell me."

"Goldman told me that they're four of us the firm's considering for partner. Since Kovac left, the firm is short one partner, if old man Grant goes ahead and retires, then there will be two openings for new partners. While it's not a shoo-in, the odds are really in my favor. And get this, due to some tax reason, they plan to make the announcement in the next few weeks, not wait 'til January like they usually do."

"Am I reading something between the lines, or is this trip going to play a big part of your chances?" At this moment Breaker, Khan, Malone, and the mystery phone number all seemed very far away.

"I think you're right on the money. We've got to get

back to National. My plane should be in soon."

***

Rick paid the taxi and they walked back into the terminal.

"Thank you again for dinner. The crab cakes were as good as I remembered."

"You're welcome. Wait for me inside and I'll check on the flight." Rick beamed when he returned. "Good news. After they took off at Chicago, they had a big tail wind from the storm and are already on the ground. We'll board in about twenty minutes. Let's go get my bag and briefcase."

Rick led them down a hall to the security check at the entrance to the locker area. Pam placed her purse on the conveyer belt and put her watch in a small plastic box. Rick placed his watch and the contents of his pockets in the same container She stepped through the electronic opening and waited until her purse came through. When she reached for her watch, she gasped and grabbed another object from the box.

"What's this?" She held a key in her shaking hand. An unusual key. It had a two-inch long shaft with notches down one side. The handle was circular brass, the size of a half dollar, stamped on each side of the handle were the numbers 422.

Rick looked at the key. "That's the locker key. What did you think it was? Your eyes got as big as a grapefruit. It didn't scare you did it?" He laughed. "Come on, we've got to get going. At this point I sure don't want to miss my flight."

***

"Rick."

"Yes." He turned and faced his wife.

"Good luck sweetheart."

"Thank you baby."

They embraced and kissed once more. Rick released her from his arms, turned and headed for the gate.

Pam stood in the empty departure area long after Rick's plane left. Over dinner all of this seemed so remote. Now she knew what the key was and tomorrow another piece of the mystery might fall into place. She wished she could forget the whole thing, but realized that was not possible. With a sigh she left the airport.

CHAPTER 17
THE LOCKER

Pam watched from the window as Ricky, Adam, and the other children boarded their bus for the last day of summer school. Tomorrow morning the boys would leave with Rick's folks for ten days of learning to fish and some good old fashioned goofing off. It certainly didn't hurt either that Liz Wilson was a first rate cook who loved to bake.

She found it difficult to believe that only six weeks ago Ricky was a basket case and that his mother had been just as bad. Only one bad dream since the middle of July and Pam didn't wake up screaming.

Her mind wandered. She planned to call Frank today and let him know how she made out with the phone call tracing. She decided the best thing to do would be to go to Reagan first and open the locker before calling him.

Driving to the airport, Pam wondered what it would contain, if anything. She remembered a few years ago somebody in a Chicago hotel discovered a hidden room that had belonged to Al Capone. After much media fanfare speculating about the contents, they opened the room and found it empty. Pam wondered about the contents of the locker. If it was empty, she wouldn't know any less than she did now. What if it contained something her parents were hiding? She would face that one if it happened.

The airport was nearly empty on Monday morning and Pam had no trouble finding a parking spot, nothing like last night. She crossed traffic to the terminal. Hiding her excitement, she went through security and into the locker area. She located number 115 and slid the key into the lock, turned it, and held her breath. The door swung open. Inside sat a slim tan leather briefcase. Acting as though this was exactly what she knew would be inside, in the event someone had watched, she removed the briefcase. Pam left the terminal carrying the case and went to her car. The plan was to take it home and open it there, but she couldn't stand the suspense. She placed the case on the front seat next to her and opened the latches. What if this damn thing explodes flashed through her mind as she slowly raised the lid and peered inside.

"What the hell's this?" She took a spiral-bound school composition book from the briefcase. Flipping through the pages she saw several with handwritten lists of numbers in her father's tight little writing, but most were blank. What was he hiding? Pam had alternated between hoping the contents of the locker might be helpful in answering who killed her parents and fearing it might support Breaker's Mafia theory. She had no idea which one she had found. She placed the book back in the briefcase, closed it, and drove home.

Back home, she studied the book closer. She was certain of her father's handwriting. Twelve pages were used. On top of each page were letters, sometimes two, sometimes three. Some pages nearly full, some with only a few entries. In the left column were four numbers, starting with either four or five. The next column contained from six to nine characters, alpha and numeric. The next column was numbers in two sets separated by a slash. Two to five numbers on one side of the slash and three to five on the other. Under each set were more numbers. The right-hand column had numbers rounded to fifty up to two hundred and fifty and followed by the letter K. On closer examination the last numbers read 50, 100, 150, 200, or 250. Her finger traced across one line.

4225   FT254671   14/1498   250K

00126586

She wondered if it represented a code of some type. Did it have something to do with their investments? If it did, why hide the briefcase and the locker key? She had no idea. Pam put the book back in the case.

She called Malone's office. He was out, but Patsy made a two o'clock appointment. She had housework to do, and needed to get Ricky's things together for his trip. But one thought would not leave her mind. What if it was true? What if somehow this was linked to something illegal that involved daddy? She could get rid of the book, nobody else knew it even existed. She had only told Patsy she needed to talk to Malone, not why. Her jaw firmed. She had come this far and could not stop, even if the truth was damning. Maybe Dutch's comments were right after all.

CHAPTER 18
THE NOTEBOOK

Patsy ushered Pam into Malone's office. He stood up and took Pam's hand, "Hi, Pam. Did you have a nice weekend? Rick get off all right?"

"The answer to both is yes."

"Patsy said you needed to see me, I had expected only a phone call, so you must have found something pretty good? Let's sit over at the table so we can spread out if need be." They walked to the table and sat down. Pam placed the tan briefcase next to her chair. She still had not decided what to do with the book.

Malone sat facing Pam and spoke first. "I talked to some Commonwealth and local police. They all buy the crack-head theory and see no reason to think otherwise. During the investigation they thought they might have something with your father's hacking into the bank computers, but when Treasury told them to back off they got miffed and dropped it. I haven't hit them yet with the fact that their best piece of evidence is a broken clock. They'll hate that, but it's not sufficient for them to reopen the case. That leaves us on our own. What do you have?"

He stopped to thumb through some papers. "No, let's talk about phone calls first."

Pam explained to Malone the possible relationship between the asterisk number and the mystery number.

"You may well have something. It could be coincidence of course. But that's unlikely, at least in my opinion. Since we believe your folks were killed between the 9:08 call and your 10:05 call, that means the mystery number could very well be the killer or at least connected to the killer. Especially if that's the same person who parked in your folk's driveway. The secure number might then link the government into this."

Pam shifted in her chair. "I take it that you're not buying the police theory at all."

"At first I had sort of an open mind, but not anymore. There are just too many pieces that don't fit into their scenario. I wish at least we knew where the secure telephone was located, that could give us a start."

"You think we have no prayer of finding out?"

"None. You tried to run down the mystery number with the phone company?"

"I talked to a supervisor but no luck."

"It's like I told you on the phone Friday, they've been burned so much in years gone by, it takes a court order to get that information now. Well let's move on, what do you have new?"

Pam placed her hand on the briefcase, hesitated, and lifted it to the table. "Frank, I've found a book, a book of my father's. I have no idea what it is. Maybe it's something that will help solve who murdered my parents. Or maybe it will prove that daddy was involved in something illegal and that what Breaker wrote was correct. I don't know if I should give it to you or not. I thought I had decided. Now, I'm not so sure."

Frank Malone rose from his chair, walked to the only

window in his office and looked out. He stood there several minutes. "Occasionally I need to look out this window to remind myself why I never look out of it. All you can see is the side of the building next door. A blank wall. Are you sure it's your father's book?"

"It's a school composition book filled with lists of numbers in his handwriting."

He stood motionless looking out the window. "Stop there, Pam. If you give me or show me the book, and it has any connection to illegal activity, I have no choice, legally, ethically, or morally; I will have to take action with it. If it turns out to be something that would only embarrass you or your family, then I suppose we could just forget it. I know I've hit the ball back into your court, but that's the way it is. I hope you're not facing a blank wall."

Malone turned and walked back to the table. "Coffee?"

"Please."

"Black wasn't it?"

"Yes."

He walked to his desk and flipped the intercom's switch. "Patsy, would you mind bringing us some black coffee?" An affirmative answer came back from the intercom. "Thank you."

Malone walked to the window again and stood there until Patsy knocked on the door.

"Here you go." Patsy walked in with two coffee mugs. One look at the expressions on Pam and Malone's faces told her everything. She put the coffee on the table and left the office.

Malone walked back to the table.

"Have you shown this to anyone else?"

"No."

They both sat in silence.

Pam's teeth closed over the edge of her lip. Her mind moved in grave deliberation. *Do the right thing, do the right thing, do the right thing. How many times did daddy say that to me? But what the hell's the right thing?* Pam sipped her coffee. With a movement of her slender shoulders she opened the briefcase and handed Malone the book. He laid it on the table between them.

"You can pick this up and take it with you if you wish. If I pick it up again, you're on a road that doesn't turn back. Your call."

"Frank, I've been through too much already to quit. If nothing else I must have faith and confidence in my parents that this all has an explanation. To take this book back now would do their memory a terrible injustice."

"You're quite a lady. You can't imagine how much I admire you." Malone picked the book up and opened it. He thumbed through several pages. "This isn't anything but lists of numbers."

"That's what I told you."

"I know that, but I didn't think it looked like this. Was your father a bookkeeper on the side?"

"No." They both laughed. "Frank, what do you think it is, what does it represent?"

"Pull your chair over here and let's see what we have. Do the letters at the top of these pages mean anything at all to you?"

"No. I've tried to tie them to something, but I can't come up with anything."

"I can't either right now. Let's go on to the lists of numbers. The first four numbers are Julian dates."

"How do you know that?"

"Here, I'll show you."

He got a calendar from his desk. "Today's August 20, the 232nd day of the year 2006. That would be written, as a Julian date, like this." He took a lined pad and a felt tip pen and wrote, 6232.

"The first digit is the year, the other three are the

sequential days of the year. December 31 last year would be five-three-six-five." He wrote again, 5365. "Does it make any sense now?"

"Yes it does. But why?"

"Without going into long explanations, it's a military shorthand way of writing dates. Very short, easy, and precise. Just the way I would imagine your dad doing it. The dates appear to start in mid 2004 and go through 5127, the last entry I see, which would be early May 2005. Less than a week before the murders." Malone stopped and cut his eyes toward Pam.

"I'm okay, so those are just dates? Probably dates when something happened?"

"That's right. But what, I have no idea. The next column's either document numbers, transaction numbers, or something like that. No idea about that either. The next column, the one with numbers separated by a slash are almost certainly bank numbers. For example the Bank of New York is fifty slash two thirty-five."

"How in the world would you know that number off the top of your head?"

"I've been working on a case where somebody forged a bunch of checks on my client's account at The Bank of New York. The numbers under the bank number are probably an account number. The last numbers are thousands of something."

"You mean like in a computer, so many K's of this and that?"

"Not today, computers deal in much bigger numbers . . ." Malone stopped in mid-sentence. He picked up the book and slowly thumbed through it. "Hey, there are twelve sections in here. Why didn't you tell me that?"

"You never asked me."

"Doesn't that ring a bell?"

Pam slowly shook her head. It seemed at times Malone

talked in circles. "No it doesn't, but it should, shouldn't it?"

"Remember, there were twelve secret files your father set up in his computer, then erased. He could have just printed the data out in hard copy. But he didn't, or at least if he did, he subsequently copied it over into this book. What a very ingenious way to hide information. A kid's composition book"

She wasn't certain why, but Pam was becoming irritated. "Where's all this leading us?"

"Now I'm not too certain. I'd want to spend more time with the book and try to pick at some of the numbers. See what might turn up. Then . . .?" Malone shrugged his shoulders.

Now Pam's thoughts crystallized. "It looks as though my father was very concerned with hiding something, doesn't it? Something he didn't want anyone to find. Maybe Breaker really has stumbled onto something. Maybe I've been stupid all along."

"What are you talking about? There's nothing here that indicates any of that. I hate to use the term, but it's all in your mind. Let's say he was into something illegal. Where's all of his ill-gotten wealth? So he bought an expensive PC. Now we know why he did that. What else did they do to indicate your parents lived way beyond their means?"

"Nothing really, I guess. They lived in that house about twenty years. The Buick was three years old and Mom's little car probably five years old. They went on a few vacations every year, either The Shenandoah Valley, or down to Hilton Head. They dressed up sometimes and went out, but that's all. I see what you mean. So much has happened, I can't always keep everything in proper context. What do we do next?"

"I'd like to have a banker look at these numbers and see what his reading would be. Do you have anyone you could take them to?"

"Not really, we bank with Northern Virginia, but Rick handles all the technical stuff with them. I just know a couple of tellers."

"How about where your dad used to work?"

"Oh, Mr. Timmons. I could see him. Let me get his number and call him from here."

"Pam, I have no idea what this book is. But I'm certain it's in someway connected with what happened to your folks. Let's play safe and handle this very low key. We'll get Patsy to copy two of the pages, two with an average number of entries. She'll certify them as 'true and correct copies' and notarize them. You take them to Timmons and tell him you found the originals among your father's papers and wondered if he could tell you what they are."

"Sure. But why am I doing it like that?"

"What do you know about Timmons?"

"Daddy worked for him a few years, but didn't think much of the man. Really, I know nothing about Timmons."

"Maybe I'm prone to overreact, but after a career working in fraud and it's many unsavory ramifications, I prefer to treat people I don't know much about very carefully. When you get home call him from your house and set up a meeting. Okay?"

"Why from my house? Why not from here?"

"I'm certain the bank has caller ID. A call from a private investigator's office is not very low key."

***

When Pam got home she dialed the bank's phone number and asked to speak to Mr. Timmons. After that she called Frank.

"Hi Patsy, may I speak to Mr. Malone, please?" Pam was glad Ricky was leaving for a while, she needed some peace and quite. "Frank, I called the bank. Timmons is in

New York until Wednesday morning. I'm on his calendar just before lunch."

"Good. I have to fly to Chicago tonight. I'll be back late Wednesday."

"No problem, I'll call you Thursday morning. Rick's in San Francisco, Ricky's going down to Petersburg, Timmons is in New York, and you're going to Chicago. It looks like I'm the only one who never has any excitement in my life. Have a good trip."

CHAPTER 19
LINDSEY'S BOOK PLACE

The storm had slackened to a steady drizzle. Pam watched water run from The Book Place's green and white stripped awning in a series of small rivers. She was bored. Bad weather meant nobody coming in and Tuesday was always slow anyway. Two sales totaling thirty dollars. Lindsey would be disappointed. Pam sat at a wooden table facing the front door, the table Lindsey used for book signings. In front of her lay the latest signing. *Silent Passion* by Merry Lowman. Like most women, Pam enjoyed a good romance novel, a good one. She doubted that Merry fell into that category. At any rate Pam had too much on her mind now to concentrate on a book, no matter how well written.

Pam picked up a pad on which she'd scribbled a list of names.

Ned Breaker
Steve Morris
Bill Lee
Philip (?)

Rajah Khan

She had erased Dutch Vortmann from her list. Pam studied the paper for a few minutes and wrote him back in.

Breaker had called her a mousy brunette. Indeed. Next to his name she wrote lounge lizard.

Steve Morris was a creep, but he did know something about what her father did on his last trip to Bangkok. He also had some idea about Vietnam, but that was probably second hand. Maybe he knew more than he told. Maybe not. He did tell Pam how to get hold of Khan, not that it did her any good. Next to his name she put three question marks.

Philip was a flunky.

She had never laid eyes on Lee or Khan.

Dutch. He could be like an uncle or a jerk.

Pam drew a wavy line across the paper and began writing again.

Key
12 files
Book
Broken clock
Car in driveway
Mystery number
*** number

Pam studied her new list for several minutes. Thoughts tried to form in her head, but nothing of substance emerged. She leaned her head back as tears formed in her eyes. She snapped her head upright and clamped her jaw shut. *Don't cry. I'm all Mom and Dad have now and I can't let them down.* Pam nearly jumped from her chair. She wrote again.

The bullet that missed Mom - a fourth bullet?

Pam stared at the now full sheet of paper. There had not been anything in the police files about a fourth bullet. She planned asking Malone about it but forgot. Pam half mumbled to herself, "When I talk to Frank Thursday, I'll have to say something."

And Dutch's comment at the Goff's party. "Be careful digging into something like this, you may not like what you find. It may not be at all what you think." What was that supposed to mean? He had called earlier this afternoon asking about an out of print book. Pam had tried to start a conversation, but he said he was on his way to a meeting. They should get together later. And then that question came back. How did Dutch know that she had been looking into what happened to her folks?

Pam put the pad down and looked at her watch. Lindsey said she might be late. With her guys gone she guessed that was okay.

Frozen pizza and *Sleepless in Seattle*, how wild could she get. The bell over the front door tinkled.

"Hi, Lindsey. You're early. I wasn't expecting you until about five. It's only three thirty now."

"No lines anywhere. I decided not to go shopping. This weather put me out of the mood. How's business, or dare I even ask?"

"Slow."

"Real slow?"

"Uh-huh."

"Real, real slow?"

"Uh-huh."

"Shit."

Pam and Lindsey laughed..

"Say, I see you're reading *Silent Passion*."

Pam blushed. "Not really. I started but just couldn't get into it."

"Don't blame you. Her stuff's mediocre but it sells like hot cakes and everybody who meets her adores her. More than one hundred so far. Take that copy if you want it. With Rick gone you may need some company tonight."

"Thanks, but I'm going to pick up an old video on the way home. That and a frozen pizza. Wow, this crazy hedonistic life style of mine is too much."

"At least I can see why women like Merry's books. In one of them her heroine's husband goes to Europe for a week and she takes six lovers while he's gone. Oops, excuse me, I forgot Rick's going to be gone for a week." Lindsey couldn't suppress a smile.

"Oh, ha ha. Sometimes I can't even handle one of 'em."

Lindsey looked at Pam's paper. "What's your list? Or is it none of my business?"

"No that's okay. I've been probing into what really happened to my folks."

"I know, you told me."

"Well, these are all of the pieces I've come up with so far. Have you ever done a jigsaw puzzle?"

"I did some when I was a kid. Is that what you have there?"

"I think so. All of this has, I'm almost certain, some connection to my parents. But I have no idea which part goes with which. With a puzzle you can sort out pieces by color and design. Here nothing fits at all. If I keep working at it, I'm hoping something will fall out. Anyway, if you don't need me, I'm off. I've already put my time down. How's the weather?"

"Not bad, still a drizzle that looks like it'll go on all night. Drive carefully. Your men calling tonight?"

"Uh-huh."

"Say hi to them for me. Bye now.

Pam left Lindsey's Book Place. She drove a few blocks to the video store where she had to wait for a parking place.

When it rained everybody had to rent a bunch of videos.

***

Back home, *Sleepless in Seattle* went on the coffee table and Pam walked into the office. There was one message on the answering machine. She hoped Ricky was okay. He wasn't supposed to call this early. She pushed the play button.

"Hey Pam, it's Lindsey. I hate to bother you, but I think I ought to tell you this. I mean with Rick out of town and you alone. Right after you left, this man came in and wanted to know if you were still here. I told him no. He wanted to know where you had gone and when. I told him I had no idea, and I didn't think it was any of his business. He looked around some. I was just about to call nine one one when he started out. Then he stopped and wanted to know if you were in the back room. I told him no, and asked him to please leave. Like I said, I hate to bother you with this, but please keep your eyes open. He's a big guy, and honey, he looked mean as the Devil. He scared the hell out of me. If you need anything call me. You have my home number. Bye now. Good luck."

What was that all about? Who in the world could it be? She listened to the message again and decided the best thing to do was turn on the security system and call the Springfield Police. They say they will make extra trips by your house if you need it.

***

At twelve fifteen Pam turned off the lamp on her night stand. Rick should call soon. Ricky called earlier. The Springfield Police called twice to check on her. She called Gabby, who called her back later. Brad pointed out that if the guy planned coming to her house, he wouldn't have let Lindsey identify him. Unless of course he was a junkie. Then all bets were off on what he might do.

Pam shook her head and sighed. *Why are people always trying to make me feel better?*

The phone rang. Pam flicked the light back on and picked up the receiver. She waited for someone to speak.

"Hi baby it's me."

"Hi Rick, I thought you had forgotten about me."

"No way. Are you okay? Have you heard from Ricky?"

She decided it would not be a good idea to mention the stalker to Rick. "Great. Worked at Lindsey's for a while, but we had a terrible storm so I came home early. Ricky called. They got there fine. He didn't talk long, Adam had to call his folks and the boys are going fishing early in the morning. What's new out there?" She felt better just talking to Rick.

"Hold on to your hat. This morning the merger hit an unexpected roadblock. The issue of generic research had never come up. The Canadians want it all paid for by the joint venture. The Japanese really don't want to pay for any of it, but will pick up the cost if it leads to a new or improved product. Our people feel about the same way. The Canadians say if there's no generic research, then new products are unlikely."

Pam loved her husband very much, but why in the world did he have to talk about this at midnight? "What happens next and when will you come home? This bed's getting bigger every night. And your wife's feet are cold."

"Just listen. We took an hour break. It looked like either the Canadians or Japanese, or both, were going to walk. I said why don't we get the three sides to form an ad hoc committee to meet when required and evaluate which research would be financed by the joint venture, either in full or in part. Are you following this?"

"As well as I'm apt to at twelve thirty at night."

Rick ignored her comment. "The bottom line would be, if the venture doesn't finance, and the research pays off, the Canadians would get double their cost back off the top. That's an inducement for two things: the Canadians to be judicious in what they propose to do, and our people and the Japanese to be more willing to buy into good research projects. I got hold of Goldman back in DC. He said go with it, things can't get any worse. We met again after lunch. And get this, they all loved the idea. That was the last big issue. We're off and running now."

"Fantastic. Good for you. I'll bet they're happy they put you in charge of this now." While Pam might not know exactly what had happened, she did know exactly what she should say.

"I don't want to keep you up any longer. But I need to tell you this. The Japanese honcho's so excited he's taking the whole team on a dinner cruise tomorrow night. The boat goes down the coast somewhere and back. We won't be in until well after midnight, so I'm not going to call tomorrow night. Is that okay?"

"Of course. Have a good dinner and again congratulations. I love you darling. Good night."

"I love you too. Good night and dream about me."

Pam switched off the light and fell asleep wondering if she would ever be able to put the jigsaw puzzle together.

CHAPTER 20
TIMMONS

*P*am was ushered into Harold Timmons' pretentious office. Wood paneled walls were covered with original oil paintings in expensive gilt frames. Timmons' walnut desk matched the oversized conference table and leather office chairs. The complete lack of clutter spoke of either extreme efficiency or inactivity.

The banker came from behind his desk to greet her. "Pam, Pam Wilson. So good to see you again. I assume you're interested in moving your accounts to our bank." He chuckled at his own attempted humor. "I haven't seen you since . . . since . . ."

"The funeral. I saw you at the Goff's party in Georgetown a month or so ago but didn't get a chance to speak."

"Yes, I remember the party. Please have a seat." He motioned her to one of the chairs facing his desk. The plush carpet yielded to her step. She selected the chair away from the door, assuming Timmons would sit facing her. He leaned against his desk, arms folded across his ample middle, obviously very ill at ease as he stared at her.

Timmons' demeanor surprised Pam. *He must be uncomfortable with me because of my parents.* She realized any conversation would start with her.

"As I said, I saw you at the party, but you were busy talking to someone, then I got tied up with Dutch Vortmann. You know Dutch don't you? His office is in this building. Before my father came to work in your bank, they worked in the same law firm together."

"Dutch Vortmann? No. I don't believe I know him at all. Would you care for some coffee, a soft drink, or anything? I've been in meetings all morning. I'll have coffee." He walked toward the door.

"No thank you."

There was something about Timmons Pam did not care for, but at the moment she was not certain what. He was pouchy, balding, and looked dissipated. And he acted as though he would be happier if she was gone when he came back. Pam took some folded papers from her purse.

She had several minutes to sit and contemplate the bank. This was a weird place with twelve teller positions, but only two tellers. Almost nobody in the lobby. Daddy used to say, "Why is that man paying me more than fifty thousand a year to bring in new customers, when he doesn't seem to care if he ever gets one?"

Timmons came back in and sat behind his desk. He looked at Pam and smiled. In a few seconds his secretary came in carrying a china cup and saucer.

"Now Pam, what can I do for you today?"

"I went through some of Daddy's old papers last week and came across these. I can't figure them out at all, and wonder if you could shed some light on what they might be? I hate to bother you, but I can't think of anyone else to ask." Pam handed the photocopied papers to Timmons.

He looked at them, front and back, and was visibly shaken. He quickly tried to regain his composure as he looked at Pam and stammered. "What . . . ah . . . what . . . ah . . . what exactly do you want me to do?" His hands shook.

"Those letters on the top of each page?"

Timmons brightened. "Ah yes. Let's see, that looks like it might be black horse." He seemed pleased with his answer.

"What's a black horse?" Pam asked.

Timmons' look appeared condescending to Pam. "Back in the old days before we had computers, retailers would write the cost of an item on the price tag using a code. Notice that black horse has ten letters none of which repeat. Going from one to zero, we could write any number in code. For example, we're selling something for eight dollars that cost us four-fifty. We would write c-k-e on the tag. C being four and so on. Understand? Today we have bar codes and all that high tech jazz."

He leaned back in his chair with obvious self-pleasure.

"What does that have to do with my father?"

"You asked me what I thought. I told you."

Pam decided to drop the letters. "This first column of numbers appear to be dates." To her amazement Timmons agreed.

"What could the second column be?" Pam asked.

Timmons studied the papers. "I have no earthly idea. Maybe just random numbers." His smile was faint. "Also the third column looks like someone making up groups of numbers. I'm not aware of it, but did your father do ciphers?"

"Do what?"

"You know, making up secret codes and such and then trying to break his own codes? Like solving the German Enigma code."

"Not that I'm aware of."

"Oh, I just wondered." He started to hand the papers

back to Pam but hesitated.

"What do you make of the last column?" Pam felt she was getting nowhere.

Timmons looked at the papers again. "That's just a measure of computer memory. Maybe each of your father's make believe codes would take up that much memory." Timmons gave Pam another condescending look.

Pam explained, as she had been told by Malone, "I didn't think computer people dealt with small numbers like that anymore."

"I really don't know, child, I'm a bank president, not a computer programmer." He smiled broadly at his own humor. Pam could feel red creeping up her neck onto her face.

Don't blush dammit. Her command did no good.

Timmons stood up, walked around his desk to Pam and handed her the pages. "I'm truly sorry I couldn't be more help. If there's anything more I can do for you, please call. We all thought the world of your parents you know."

When Pam stood up, Timmons subtlety edged her to the door. "Good day now." The banker's hand on Pam's waist still trembled.

"Thank you Mr. Timmons," Pam commented to a closing door. She nodded to his secretary and left the office.

As Pam stalked through the door leading from the bank to the building lobby, she fumed. *What a pompous stupid ass. Does he really think I'm that dumb?* Pam was so engrossed with her thoughts, she nearly ran head on into a man entering the lobby.

"Excuse me! Oh Dutch, I almost plowed into you."

"I saw you coming, but I didn't dodge quick enough." Dutch laughed. "What's up?"

"Just doing some banking."

"I didn't know you banked here."

"We don't, I happened to be in the area." Pam realized her answer sounded lame. She should say something intelligent now. "Did you find that book you called The Book Place about?"

"Huh?"

"You remember, the one you called about yesterday morning when I was working. I told you it was out of print, but maybe Lindsey could find a copy of it for you. She very good at finding those old books."

"Oh yeah, yeah, that book. Now I remember. It's about lunchtime. Want to grab something to eat?"

"Why not." Dutch's vagueness about the book surprised her. Yesterday he had made it sound so important.

"If we hurry, we can get in Cousins before the crowd. Let's take my car. I want to show it off."

***

Timmons breathing returned to normal and his hands stopped shaking before he dialed his private telephone. He listened for a few seconds. "I need to talk to him." A pause. "Well, when will he get back?" Pause. "No, I'll call again later." Harold Timmons placed the receiver in its cradle and pressed his head into his folded arms as he leaned forward across his desk.

***

"This is some swanky car."

"So much better to pick the chicks up with my dear."

Pam suppressed a smile. *Do guys ever grow up? He's as old as my father.*

"I've always wanted a Beemer, now I have one. Life's too short to deprive yourself. The Lincoln I had was a great car, but you look around and it seems like everybody has a gold-colored Lincoln. And they sure don't pick up the babes too good."

Pam rolled her eyes and said nothing.

Dutch guessed correctly. They beat the usual crowd. Cousins sat in the center of one of the busiest areas of Alexandria. Its sleek interior and excellent food attracted yuppies and wannabes by the droves. After being seated they ordered Dutch's favorite lunch. Sliced tenderloin over a toasted English muffin, topped with sautéed mushrooms and hunter sauce. Before the waiter left their table, Dutch looked at Pam. "Would you care for a drink?"

"No thanks."

"Dry martini, straight up."

Dutch turned back to Pam. "Well little one. How's your family? It's a shame we can't see more of each other. Ricky will be in college before I ever get to know him."

Pam wondered how he could be such a sweet person one minute and the next minute so cruel. "Great. Rick's on an important business trip to California. It has new partner written all over it. Ricky's down with the Wilson's learning how to fish and, I'm afraid, getting completely spoiled by his grandparents."

The small talk continued. Dutch was still moving into his new condo, a lot of boxes not yet unpacked. During the discussion their lunch arrived and Dutch ordered another martini.

"Considering how little bachelors have, moving in should take thirty minutes. But then I told you all that at the Goff's that night. You may not remember. You did get a little smashed." He smirked at Pam and patted her hand.

Pam felt quite certain she was not the first woman Dutch Vortmann had gotten drunk. They ate in silence until Pam placed her fork on her plate.

She looked directly at Dutch. "That night, do you

remember telling me about the first pistol shot that missed my mother?"

"No, I never told you anything like that." They had finished eating. Dutch caught the waiter's attention and pointed to his glass.

"Yes you did. You even went on about what happened to you in Vietnam and how she must have felt knowing the next one would hit her, or something like that."

"Pam, you must have been much drunker that night than I thought."

"No Dutch, I remember distinctly what you told me. I could never forget that. It was - -"

"You're getting very damn irritating." Dutch slammed down his still empty glass. He stood up and threw two twenty-dollar bills on the table. "Come on. I've got work to do this afternoon."

Dutch stormed from the restaurant with Pam hurrying after him. They drove back to the bank in silence.

"Where's your car?"

"Over there. The dark green SUV. Dutch, I'm sorry I went on like that. It was uncalled for."

"That's okay, Pam. I'm just off my feed or something. Don't worry about it. I'll catch you and Rick later."

Pam got out of the BMW and walked to her car. She watched Dutch pull into a space marked Vortmann, leave his car and walk somewhat unsteadily to the office building. Pam unlocked her door and slowly slid into the driver's seat. Deep in thought, she bit her lip with no regard to getting lipstick on her teeth.

CHAPTER 21
JOAN BURRIS

"I am a certified, gold-plated, four star jerk! First I go see Harold Timmons with legitimate questions and he treats me like a dim-witted twelve-year-old. Then the guy who's supposed to be my friend and knew my father for forty years lies to me and has a temper tantrum. Just how am I going to act?" Pam talked aloud as she drove on King Street toward Interstate 395.

"Anyway, I know he lied. He made a point of making that first bullet so grotesque it was almost unbearable and then telling about being shot at in Vietnam. And I wasn't drunk when he told me that. Maybe later, but certainly not then."

Pam drove in silence, at least she had that off her chest, she thought. The Interstate was just ahead. A turn right would take her to the beltway, then to Springfield and home. She slid into the left lane and turned north onto Interstate 395. This direction would take her, among other places, to Mount Vernon. The only way she could answer this was to go to her folk's house and look for herself. Could she do it? Pam's eyes watered, "Hell yes I can do it!"

At Glebe Road Pam turned right, toward Mount Vernon. She pulled into the driveway of 2475 Miles Street, turned off the engine, and sat in her car. This had been her parents' home for two decades. Her heart pounded like a jackhammer. She had not set foot in the house since May 13, 2005. What if their bodies were still on the floor? What if she knocked on the door and one of them answered? She sat motionless in the front seat of her car hyperventilating. Pam squeezed her eyes shut. Before her a vision of her father floated. He had that silly grin on his face and his right hand in front of his chest. He gave her his thumbs up. Pam took several deep breaths. With slow, agonizing moves she got out of her car, walked to the front door and rang the bell.

Joan Burris opened the door. Joan was a small, white haired, woman in her sixties. Pam sighed with relief and introduced herself again. They had met once in the attorney's office for the closing.

"I really hate to bother you, but would it be all right if I looked around the house for something?"

"Child, no bother at all. Come on in." Joan Burris' smile belied her nervousness. As Pam walked through the house, Joan constantly stayed between her and a door. She seemed to expect any second Pam would rush her brandishing a weapon. She was ready to run in an instant. Pam noticed this, but had no idea why the older woman acted that way.

Pam walked into the living room. The carpet had been replaced. That would make sense, it was ten years old anyway. She walked around where her father had died. With a deep breath she stepped to the kitchen door.

"You've redone this haven't you?"

"Yes, dear." Joan's extreme embarrassment showed as she groped for words. "Well, yes, actually that is, ah . . . well it seemed like the best thing to do under the circumstances."

The tile, cabinets, and counters were all new and the walls had been repainted. "Other than the kitchen and the carpet, have you and Mr. Burris done anything else?"

"No. The furniture's all ours, of course. The walls had been repainted only a year or so before we bought the house so we didn't do anything to them. No, everything else is about the same." Joan continued to eye Pam carefully and stayed out of reach.

Pam stepped into the kitchen. With another deep breath she looked at where her mother's body had lain. Pam was surprised she could study the scene and think clearly about what had happened.

Her mother must have run from the living room or the bedroom into the kitchen, directly toward the archway to the dining room, and then for the side door to the driveway. Someone must have shot her while she ran. Pam raised her hand and aimed her finger in the form of a mock handgun. Her finger pointed through the archway toward a dining room wall, to where a woven hemp wall hanging was displayed, the one her father brought from Thailand on that infamous last trip.

"You said you haven't painted any of the walls?"

"No, none."

"Have you ever taken that wall hanging down?"

"No. The realtor said it came with the house. We both liked it so we left it on the wall. If you want it Pam, please feel free to take it with you. We certainly will understand if you do."

"No, I don't want it, but do you mind if I take it down from the wall?"

Before Joan Burris could give her assent, Pam had the hanging on the dining room table. Directly in the middle of the wall was a dark streak and a gouge in the Sheetrock. Pam felt the deepest end of the gouge and found a hole, a very small hole. The killers used a twenty-two-caliber pistol. The hole seemed about that size.

"Joan do you have a utility knife I could use?"

Without understanding why, Joan brought a knife from the garage and handed it to Pam.

Working with careful movements, Pam dug into the Sheetrock. The knife cut easily through plaster. Then she hit a stud. Slowly she picked away the wood, one sliver at a time. Then she stopped. Using the end of the knife she pried a lump of metal from the wall. She was no ballistics expert, but this certainly looked like a beat up twenty-two slug. Pam took out a tissue, placed her prize in it, and put the folded tissue back in her purse. Joan had watched the entire process in a state of shock.

"Mrs. Burris, I'm sorry about this mess. I'll have someone come out this week to clean it up and patch the wall."

"That's all right dear. Did you find what you were after?"

"Yes, I believe I did."

Joan Burris watched as Pam drove away. When the car moved out of sight, the older woman walked to the telephone.

***

Harold Timmons slumped in a chair. His eyes glazed and his chin sagging. "I knew this would happen."

"Will you shut your damn mouth. How do you know that wasn't just a couple of pieces of paper she found squirreled away in her father's things? That's what she said it was."

"I've already told you. Someone named Patsy had authenticated the back of both pages."

"Maybe they took the old pages and recopied them?"

"Yeah, maybe they did that, maybe they did. You're the ambulance chaser, why would they put a fingerprint on a copy of a copy. Why would they do that? Why would they do that? You know as damn well as I do!"

"Lower you voice before somebody hears you."

Timmons continued unabated. "You know why . . . so it can be admitted as evidence!"

"Okay, okay. You go back down to your office and let me mull this over. I'll call the boss and get back with you."

Harold Timmons pulled himself to his feet, sighed, and slowly left the office. As soon as the door closed, the red telephone rang.

"Yes?"

"It's me. I'm not saying my name like you told me."

"Well good for you. I'm busy as hell, what do you want?"

"Just like you said, she came here, she's half crazy too. Took a wall hanging down that belonged to her mother. Then she cut a hole in my wall. Left a general mess on the floor. She took something out of that hole, wrapped it up in a tissue and took it with her."

"Shit."

***

The drive home should have taken no more than twenty-five minutes, but in rush hour she had crawled along for more than forty minutes. Halfway home it had come to her again. The scrap of conversation she couldn't forget, but also could not understand completely. "I understand you've been nosing around about what happened to you folks?" Those were Dutch's words. How did he know what she had been doing?

When Pam got home she went to the hall closet and took out the envelopes she had taken from the attic the day she dropped her mother's jewel box.

"I know that it's in here, I've seen it before. Ah ha. This is it."

She held her father's well-used address book. Pam walked into Rick's office and took a file folder from a stack on the floor. She fumbled through the contents and extracted a lone sheet.

"Well here goes absolutely nothing."

Dutch had moved six months ago so maybe his old phone number would be in her father's address book. Maybe he didn't even bother writing it down. She opened the book to the U V section. Underwood, Uncle Lester, Varsey, Victor. No Vortmann. She guessed she was just as happy, it had been a long shot anyway. Idly she flipped to the D section. There it was:

Dutch **555-0464.**

Pam's hands shook when she picked up the caller ID sheets. The number that called four times on Thursday and Friday, including the 9:08 call on Friday night was.........555-0464.

CHAPTER 22
THE CONVERSATION

"How many times do I have to tell you people not to call me on this number?"

"Isn't this your green phone? This line's supposed to be secure."

"Nothing in Langley's secure. Where are you?"

"In my office."

"Stay there. I'll call you in about twenty minutes."

***

"Now slowly and carefully tell me just what is going on to get you so riled up. Have you been drinking?"

"Hey, it's the middle of the afternoon."

"I didn't ask what time it is, I want to know if you're bombed out or not."

"Hell no! Dammit!"

"Good, go ahead."

"There are actually a couple of things. The first one's that Pam Wilson took copies of two pages from Anders' book to Timmons."

"What? Why?"

"She asked him if he could figure out what the columns of numbers were. He gave her some Timmons gobbledygook and she left. She said she was going through some of her father's papers and found them. She said she couldn't think of anyone else to ask."

"Whose sheets were they?"

"Timmons forgot to look."

"Figures. Why do you two think they're from the book instead of what Wilson said?"

"Timmons said they were authenticated on the back."

"You mean 'this is a true and accurate' and so forth?"

"Yeah. They were signed by Patsy somebody and date/timed."

"How do you know they weren't our sheets?"

"According to Timmons there were only about fifteen to twenty entries on each page."

"OK shyster, what are the chances someone would certify a copy of a copy?"

"Not likely, but possible."

"So we really don't know whether she has the book or not, do we?"

"No. How much chance can we take?"

"Not a whole lot, that's for sure. How did Timmons handle it?"

"From what he said and the way he acted with me later, I'd say he just about lost it."

"So now we have the possibility that if he gets leaned on, or if someone figures out whose sheets those are, we've got three people who could squeal on us. To save their butt they'd turn on the rest of us like Bill Lee did on Khan. You said there were two things, what's the other one. I assume it's not good news either."

"Wilson went to her parents' old house and dug that other bullet out of the wall."

"What the shit. You know you have to be the absolute dumbest SOB I've ever had the misfortune to hook up with. Why in the hell did you ever tell her about that other bullet?"

"Look, by now I sure figured somebody would have found the damn thing. At that point we wanted to make the whole affair so gruesome she'd back off nosing around. Who would have thought she would remember what I said the rest of her life."

"Where was the bullet?"

"It lodged behind a wall hanging in the dining room."

"Crap. Your babbling has me a little mixed up. Give me a chronology."

"She sees Timmons late this morning, leaves him and runs into me on her way out of the building. Tells me she's there doing some banking. I know that's a bunch of BS. I take her to lunch to find out what she's doing, if anything. She keeps going on about a fourth bullet. I tell her that I never said that, but she won't let it go. I finally get pissed off and we leave. Back at the office I see Timmons. He tells me about the pages and what he told her. He no sooner walks out of my office than Joan Burris calls, she and her husband bought the Anders' old house, telling me Wilson found the bullet. Then I called you."

"Let me do a little risk assessment here." He paused for several minutes. "Wilson may or may not have the book. If she has the book, she may or may not know what it is. In either case if she has it she will probably give it to someone else to look at. There's a good chance a knowledgeable person, not even necessarily an expert, could decipher what's in it. We may very easily end up with any number of people who could, and probably would, turn on us. I trust all the rest of you just about as far as I can throw my house. The bullet. It's her word against yours as to what you said. But it could be enough to get the case reopened, not by the police, don't think they would be happy about not finding the bullet themselves. More likely a DA, or something. Last time the law missed a lot of stuff. I can't believe we could possibly be that lucky again." Another lengthy pause.

"Well Sherlock, what did you end up with?" Vortmann asked.

"The chances of this going down bad are too great for us to live with. We're going to talk to Mrs. Wilson. How long has it been since she left Burris?"

"It's been a good hour now."

"I'll call her. Either Elliot or I will let you know the time."

"Your place?"

"Of course."

CHAPTER 23
COBRA I

*P*am sat at the desk. Before her lay her father's address book, the sheets of paper, and a mangled lump of metal. She planned going over all of this with Frank when he got back in town, he would know what to do next. She was massaging her temples when the telephone rang.

"Hello?"

"Pam Wilson?"

"Yes."

"You may not remember me. I met you at the Vice-President Goff's party in Georgetown a couple of months ago. My name's Mark Harris."

"Yes sir, I remember you." Yes she did, the CIA guy who lied about attending the funeral. Cobra with the pink glasses.

"I understand you have been doing some checking into the facts surrounding your parents' death? Is that correct?"

"That's true. It seems everyone knows it."

Harris ignored her sarcasm. "I've come across some information I believe will be of great value to you. Because of its source, I must keep passing this to you in strict confidence. I'm certain you understand why."

"Yes, go ahead." Pam did not understand at all.

"Would it be possible for us to meet later this evening?"

"I believe so, when and where?"

"Let's see, it's five forty-five, how about seven at my residence?"

"Where do you live?"

"Out toward Reston, take Highway Seven from the Beltway, go under the Dulles toll road for five and a half miles, on your left is Kennedy Creek Road, turn, go another mile. I'm on your left, 5400 Kennedy Creek. There's a wall surrounding the property, but the gate's open. Please come to the front door."

Pam scribbled directions as Cobra talked. "Could we make it a little later? Say seven thirty or eight?" she asked.

"Certainly, eight o'clock would be fine."

"Thank you. I'll see you then."

Pam was still in Rick's office. She stared at the bullet and her father's address book, both still lying on the desk blotter. *Well, guess I'd better get my butt going.* Pam picked up the telephone and began dialing.

***

She followed Harris' directions, Kennedy Creek Road, 5400, the wall, the gate, all just like he said. Pam drove through the open gate. To her left a circular drive hooked to the front door. Directly in front of her was an empty parking area for maybe six cars. Beyond that stood a low brick wall with a wooden gate in the center. Behind the wall she saw a well-manicured rose garden. In the failing light she could see the wall behind the garden was glass, with a French door to the left. She turned and backed her car up to the brick wall. After turning off the ignition, she slipped the keys under the edge of the driver's seat and walked across the gravel drive toward the house.

The front door was massive. She pushed the bell and heard deep throated chimes. In seconds the door opened. A large swarthy man with wavy black hair filled the doorway. He was not the sort you would want to meet in a dark alley.

"Wilson?"

"Yes." It appeared to her there were no pleasantries at Mark Harris' house.

"This way." They entered a hallway. Stairs to the left, doors to the right. At the first door they stopped. The man knocked and received a muffled reply. He opened the door a few inches. "Wilson's here."

"Show her in Elliot, please."

Elliot pushed the door open and jerked his head for Pam to enter. She stepped in and the heavy wooden door closed behind her. The room was massive, half again as big as her living room. On the far wall there was an oversized wet bar, well stocked with bottles, a refrigerator, ice maker, glasses, and who knew what else. To her left ran a wall of built-in bookcases. To her right was a wall of ceiling to floor drapes. On the right end of that wall, a small gap in the drapes showed the edge of the French door she had seen from outside. Behind her, the wall was adorned with several oversized paintings. The focal point of the room sat in its center, a large mahogany desk. Scattered around the room, were several leather arm chairs. The only lights in the room came from florescent tubes above the wet bar and a flexible gooseneck lamp on the desk. The room smelled of leather and old books.

"Pam, it's good of you to join us. I'm getting some wine, would you care for a glass? It's French. And at fifty bucks a throw, it better be good."

It was painfully obvious Mark Harris rarely made idle small talk.

"No thank you." Pam walked to the French door. "From what I saw when I drove up, you have a beautiful rose garden."

"Thank you. I have a service out once a week. They take care of the lawn and the plants. You're quite certain about the wine?"

Pam noted Mark Harris was not used to people telling him no.

Pam watched Harris as he turned to pour his wine. Her hand closed on the door handle and pushed. It didn't move. *Damn.* Harris turned around. "You know, Mr. Harris, I think I could go for a glass of wine."

He turned back to pour Pam's wine. Her fingers felt for the latch. She found it and slowly pushed. It clicked. The sound was lost to Harris who was busy at the bar. She pushed the handle down hoping he did not have a security system engaged. The handle moved and the door opened slightly. Pam pulled it shut as Harris turned to face her again.

"Here you go. Now please take a seat. Someone will join us, but he's late."

Pam selected a chair directly in front of the desk as Harris sat down behind it. She put her glass on an end table and never touched it again. She couldn't help wondering if he had put something in the wine. They sat for several minutes in silence. With his pink tinted glasses, Pam couldn't tell if he was looking at her or not. Her face began to flush as she desperately tried to think of something intelligent to say. "Mr. Harris, this is really an impressive house."

"Pam, please stop calling me Mr. Harris. You make me feel very old and stodgy, my name's Mark."

"Didn't I hear you called 'Cobra' at the Goff's party?"

"Yes you did. That was my code name at one time and I still like it. If you wish, you may call me Cobra." Harris smiled one of his rare smiles.

His name was appropriate, he looked as though he could strike in a second.

"Thank you, Cobra, I feel flattered." Silence descended again. Pam nervously crossed and uncrossed her legs. "You said you have information for me?"

"Yes. I'm waiting for our other guest, but we may as well start." Harris leaned forward on his desk, facing directly at Pam. "You're entitled to know why I asked you here tonight. First, your interest in what happened to your parents is understandable. That article Ned Breaker wrote contained trash, absolute filth. Whatever differences your father and I may have had in no way diminished his stature. He was a man you can remember with pride."

A knock sounded on the door. With some degree of irritation Harris answered. "Yes Elliot."

The door cracked. "He's here."

Pam could hear the door creak and someone walk into the room. "Hello Cobra, Pam."

Pam gasped. "Dutch?"

"Good evening Dutch. You're late, but then what else is new?"

Dutch ignored the comment. "Mind if I fix a drink?"

"No." Cobra looked back at Pam. "We're just getting started. You haven't missed anything."

Dutch sat down in a chair further away from the desk than Pam. She couldn't see him without turning around.

"I hope you realize," Harris continued, "that we have done almost everything humanly possible to dissuade you from pursuing this venture of yours."

"What do you mean?"

"At the Goff's, Dutch was as cruel to you as he's capable of being, and warned you that what you might find will not be what you want to find. Then Elliot went through your house. He was looking for something, which he can do without destroying your house, and he left a few clues behind to let you know just how vulnerable you really are. We hoped that would be enough. When it wasn't, yesterday Elliot waited for you to leave work. On your way home, he planned forcing your SUV into some parked cars. When he saw the local police checking the license number of the stolen car he was using, he had to ditch it. When he got back, you had left. So he went in and shook up your girl friend. I'm certain she must have called you. Right?"

Pam nodded.

"Oh yes. We had Dutch call the bookstore to make certain you were there. Now, you may be wondering why we went to all this trouble."

Pam slid to the edge of her chair and leaned toward Cobra, blood pounding in her temples. "You rotten bastard, why did you do this to me?"

Cobra recoiled from Pam's outburst. His expression turned grim as he worked to contain his anger. "If you can control your childish little temper, we can get to the meat of this."

Pam glared at him as she leaned back in her chair.

"Back in Vietnam, nineteen seventy-one, I was a station chief with the CIA. There were four of us, another with the CIA, one with State, and one with the Agency for International Development, AID. That's the organization your dad was with years later."

"I know."

"We were doing penny-anti deals, maybe five grand a year. Then I found out this Indian, Rajah Khan, planned a big time hit on the US Treasury during an MPC conversion. Five million or more. He was working with the Koreans. That left the door wide open for us. We could go for a hundred thousand each and nobody would ever notice it. Gravy. We lined up all the bar owners, hookers, and drug pushers in our provinces to exchange their ill-gotten MPC at fifty cents on the dollar. When it happened, we paid off ten cents on the dollar, take it or leave it." This time Harris' laughter was genuine.

"Stop for a minute. I need another drink." Dutch walked to the wet bar. His unsteady gait made Pam suspect he had more to drink since lunch. "Mind if I turn off this light over your fancy wet bar? It's right in my eyes."

"If it makes you happy, go ahead."

Harris waited until Dutch sat back in his chair.

"Well, we all got greedy, went for about five hundred thousand plus each. We didn't know that somehow your father had set Khan up. Two days before the conversion Khan moved all of his illegal money in place and the Army busted him. Lost all of it. This Army officer had sold us the right conversion date so we went ahead with our operation. Afterwards, we stuck out like flashing red lights. Where the hell did all that money come from? Your father headed up an investigation and came after us for blood. He believed we had done something wrong and should be punished. All of our careers would have been ruined. Then he got transferred back to the states."

"I remember, that's when we went to Indian Town Gap. I was just a kid then."

"Whatever, whatever." With a look of irritation, Harris stood and walked to the wet bar. "Another glass of wine?"

"No."

Harris returned to his desk. "With your old man gone, they brought in Dutch to finish the investigation. He could smell illegal money, and wanted a piece of the action. Now there were five of us. A few months later Dutch issued a report that said nothing, but everyone had forgotten about it by then anyway." Harris took a sip of his wine.

Over her right shoulder Pam could hear the tinkle of ice in Dutch's glass. The only light now came from the lamp on Harris' desk. The contrast of light from Cobra's lamp and the dark corners of the library created a chiaroscuro effect in the room. It reminded Pam of a mausoleum she and her parents had visited in Europe. All that the scene lacked was the musty odor of death.

CHAPTER 24
COBRA II

Harris put his now empty glass on the desk. He cleared his throat and began talking again.

Pam's anger subsided. Replacing it was an undefined fear that something was dreadfully wrong with this meeting.

"Time went by. We were all back in the DC area, doing nickel and dime junk. Your father had retired from the Army. I guess he fooled around for a year or so, and got bored. He said something to Dutch about looking for a position and Dutch called me. When you've been in this business as long as I have, you get gut feelings. We were getting due for something to happen. What, when, or where, I had no idea. But I wanted to be prepared. Bill Anders had one of the finest analytical minds I have ever seen. Probably the best person in the world to have as a point man when something breaks. I got him a five-year contract with the AID to work economic development in Southeast Asia."

Dutch got another drink, but this time Harris continued talking.

"Then three things happened, one after another, bang, bang, bang." He punctuated the events by jabbing his finger in the air three times. "First, back then Dutch and Harold Timmons were big drinking buddies. An accountant friend of Timmons had a brainstorm. It was as old as the hills, but nobody bothered with it any more.

"I won't bore you with details. You have an offshore charitable trust fund that makes distributions to accounts in the US. Since the money's foreign source, it's not reported by the trust to the IRS. In those days banks only had to report transactions like this when the amount exceeded fifty thousand. His idea was to have a dozen trusts, each with a dozen accounts. All of a sudden you're now talking big money. But it would be a very slow way to do it. Would it work? We had no idea. Also we weren't willing to use our money to try it, just in case it blew up.

"Then the second thing happened. I'm certain someone must have told you about the World Bank and other organizations clamping down on the money launderers?"

"Yes, Steve Morris told me about that."

"Good. The third event was like money from home. Did Steve also tell you about how your father saved Rajah Khan's ass by converting two hundred fifty-thousand dollars for him?"

"Yes he did. But why would Khan have anything to do with my father after what happened in Vietnam?"

"Two reasons." Harris again sounded irritated. "First, Khan liked your dad and believed he had been hoodwinked too. Bill Lee was the one who didn't trust your father. The second reason was that they were desperate. Khan's organization was going down the tube. He needed money so badly he would have done business with the Pope. Now, did that answer your question? Do you have any more before I continue?"

"Frankly Mr. Harris, you're starting to get very tedious.

What are you trying to say?"

"Kindly shut your damn mouth and listen."

Pam's face turned crimson, but she resisted a sharp retort.

"All we needed now was some business. That's where your father came to our aid. I told him we were trying to shut down Khan's operation. His deal with Morris would be a key part of our effort. Your father never came in contact with Khan, he dealt with Bill Lee. We ran their money through the offshore trusts the accountant set up. To make it even cleaner they all used Dutch's trust company to get the money in the US. Timmons' bank made the actual transfers to Khan's accounts. It worked like a well-oiled machine. When Anders got back from Bangkok, he had tapes of Lee bragging about their North American operation, drugs, prostitution, extortion. A dirty operation. They had an entire floor plus in south Manhattan just for the money operations. I believe you went up there recently didn't you?"

"Yes, but it isn't very big now." Pam wondered if there was anything she had been doing they didn't know about.

"We needed Lee to come to the States so we could nab him. After your father laundered their money, time passed, the heat came off and everything opened up again. They didn't need Anders anymore. In fact, like I said, Lee had never trusted him. I pulled your father back to the States to a desk job. Then out of the blue Morris calls your dad. Lee had sent Morris to Maryland to do something for Khan.

"Morris figured your father had a piece of something illegal too, and Morris wouldn't mind doing a little business with him if there was any money in it. Your father tipped me off that Morris had come to this country. Your dad thought we were still after Khan. We put a tap on Morris' phones and waited.

"In a couple of months he gets a call from Lee who's

coming to the states, first to Frisco, then DC, then New York. We tie in with the FBI. When Lee walks out of customs in San Francisco International, the Feds grab him. I think, if he had tried, Lee could have beaten it. All we had was an illegal tape and a few documents. But he didn't even try, folded up like a wet noodle. He had his address book in his suitcase. Gave the FBI forty plus names, phone numbers, some addresses, all the key players in Khan's North American organization. We told the FBI we had moles working on this we had to protect. They gave us the list without looking at it. Steve Morris was on it. If they talked to him, he would tell them about Bill Anders, if they talked to Bill Anders he would tell them about Mark Harris. So we took Morris off the list. In less than six months the FBI had hit almost everyone on the list. They destroyed Khan's North American operation." Harris paused. "Have I lost you with all of this?"

"No, not really. I don't understand it all, but I follow what's going on." Harris had been talking for over an hour. Pam felt that sooner or later he would get to the point and lead up to a big climax. Harris did not seem the type man who would waste this much time in idle chatter. Pam wiggled in her seat, but Cobra ignored her.

"We went to work. Our concern about how slowly the plan moved money proved correct. With a limit of fifty thousand on each transaction, and only so many transactions we could do without attracting too much attention, we were spinning our wheels.

"The organization had to expand. There were seven of us, the five from Vietnam days, Timmons, and his accountant friend. We added a senior IRS guy from Estates and Trusts and a senator and a congressman. Both of the politicians were senior on the Taxation Subcommittees in each house. Our IRS man testified to Congress that the fifty thousand dollar limit was unrealistic. Better to make it two hundred-fifty thousand, with any one transaction over that subject to a detail audit by the IRS. Our politicians ran the bills through as riders to some popular legislation. I don't even remember what. Both houses passed the bill without debate and the President signed it."

Harris leaned back in his chair for the first time and appeared to relax. "With that stroke of genius our volume had increased five fold. The next year we moved better than five million dollars. And that was just our cut. We needed one more person on the team. Someone high enough in Treasury to protect Timmons and his bank in the event auditors or whoever might nose around. Later we added another senator. But that was it, the twelve of us." Harris leaned forward again.

Dutch walked to the wet bar, turned on the light and fixed himself still another drink. "Either one of you need anything?" When he received no reply, he turned out the light, walked unsteadily to his chair, and sat down again.

"You talk about getting a senator, getting a congressman, getting a this or that; it's like you're hiring a yard service to work on your roses."

"In this city when you sit down with somebody and talk about one, two, maybe three million a year, cash, tax free, no risk, they listen. They listen very intently. Nobody ever turned us down." He thought for a minute. "Well, only one person turned us down."

Dutch spoke from behind her shoulder. "Ah Pam, Pam, you naive, innocent thing. You are your father's child aren't you?"

Her body became taut and her jaw clamped shut. *I would really love to punch Dutch in the face.* In the semi-darkness the men could not see the crimson return to her face.

"After he finished with AID", Harris spoke again, "we wanted to keep our eye on Bill Anders. He knew too much, but at the same time he wasn't aware of the significance of what he knew."

Pam wondered what he said. Was he still speaking English? Maybe it was the CIA way of saying something by not saying anything intelligible.

"Dutch got him in the law firm with an office right next door to him. That proved a mistake. In a few years, your father realized the only real client Dutch had was the trust company. Then he started asking questions. Asking the wrong questions. Why have a trust company that only handles distributions from offshore charitable trusts and foundations?

"That's when we had Timmons offer him the position as a Vice President. He was to market retired senior military officers and get them to move their banking business to Timmons' bank. Great job, good pay, he was his own boss, flexible hours, unlimited expense account. Hell, he had it made. We forgot about him and went on with the business of making money, lots of money." He paused again, thought for a few minutes and continued.

"Now we get to the unpleasant part. After three years with the bank, about sixteen months ago, your father walked into Dutch's office and handed him a piece of paper. It had Dutch's initials on the top and it listed some thirty of his money transactions. Date, document number, bank account it went into, and the amount. Before Dutch could recover from the shock, Anders handed him another paper. Mine. Your father told him that he had identified all twelve of us. He had begun back in two thousand four somehow digging into the bank's records.

"He got better, bought a powerhouse computer, and hacked into the bank's files. He worked on this from his house at nights and on weekends. The end product was damning. And, being your father, he copied the data off by hand and erased his computer files. Now he had the trump card and we wouldn't even know where to look for it. I think he believed he had bought himself a life insurance policy. If anything happened to him, whoever had the book would turn it over to the Feds."

Pam's head swam, she felt ice water in the pit of her stomach, her mind raced on a roller coaster at breakneck speed through a black void in space. *I have that book. Oh my God, I have that book. And if Timmons is in on this, they know I have it.* Pam took several deep breaths and nervously chewed on her lip.

"That was a Wednesday. He told Dutch that if we didn't turn ourselves in, he would go to the FBI with what he had. Pam, I want you to believe that no one ever meant any harm to your father or your mother. Everyone who knew them liked and respected them. He didn't realize that before Khan, someone else was doing this. After we're gone, someone will be doing it again. What we were doing was clean. We laundered money, period. We were expensive, but we worked with small fish who had no options. If you had a counterfeit one hundred-dollar bill, wouldn't you trade it for a good fifty? That's all we did. Whoever came next would probably be back into selling drugs to grade school kids."

Dutch interrupted. "Keep going. You're starting to preach."

"It's amazing, the more he has to drink, the more he runs his mouth. Anyway, Dutch told your dad he had to talk to me and that we would do something on Thursday. On Thursday we both called him. I reminded him of who the twelve were, that it was going to take time to get to all of them and formulate a plan. Your dad gave us until Friday."

Those mystery phone calls. Pam moved uneasily in her chair. She realized these two were in this up to their necks.

"On Friday I called him and convinced him to wait

until Monday. Made him an offer no sane person could possibly refuse. We would take care of him and Betty for the rest of their lives and take care of you and your family also. He said hell no. He just didn't realize that the men in on this have too much at stake to walk into a police station and surrender. Dutch wanted one more shot at talking sense to your father.

"We almost stripped Timmons' vault, but we came up with one hundred fifty-thousand dollars in used fifties and hundreds, and another fifty thousand in negotiable instruments. This being only the first installment. We would also put a half a million in a Swiss bank account for them every year. Late Friday evening, Dutch put the money and securities in a briefcase and went to your folks' house." Harris paused and moved uncomfortably in his chair.

"Did you really believe my father would take a bribe like that?"

"No, I guess not." Harris stopped talking and began tapping his desk with a silver letter opener.

With his tinted glasses, Pam wasn't certain if Cobra was looking at her, at Dutch, or what. Her mind swirled out of control again when it hit her. *Was Dutch at my parent's house on Friday night? What did their neighbor say . . . 'a big car, probably American, gold or light brown' . . . Dutch's gold-colored Lincoln!*

Pam's voice trembled with rage as she spoke. "Was Dutch at my parent's when they were killed?"

The tapping stopped.

"Well?"

Dutch cleared his throat to the tinkling of ice cubes. "You may as well go ahead and finish. If she hasn't figured it out already, it's only a matter of time until she does. And when she does the shit's gonna hit the fan. Let's get it over with now."

Cobra leaned forward as he spoke. "What should have

happened Friday night was that your dad would tell Dutch to get out and he would. Instead, Dutch had been drinking. They had a confrontation and when he realized your father was not going to buy our offer, but go to the Feds on Monday morning, Dutch lost his cool. He had carried a twenty-two-caliber automatic pistol with him. Your father finally said the wrong thing. With no warning, Dutch shot him in the head. Betty heard the noise and came out of the bedroom to see her husband lying on the floor with Dutch standing over him. She bolted for the side door. Unfortunately, Dutch had to finish her off too. He looked, tore the house up, but he couldn't find the book that night."

Pam was in a state of complete shock. She had guessed Dutch knew more about what happened than he had ever said, but never that he had killed them himself. For a few seconds, nausea overcame her. Her emotions were far too high for tears.

Cobra leaned back against his chair. "Now I hope you understand why we must have that book. There's too much at stake. You're going to take us to where it is, give us the book and any copies you have made, and then you can forget this evening and get on with the rest of your life."

Pam sat in her chair like a rock. Her thoughts were unbelievably calm. *Two months ago I'd be bawling my eyes out, listening to how my parents were shot down in cold blood. Now all I want is to destroy these bastards.* She opened her mouth to speak, but Cobra interrupted her.

"I do hope you realize Elliot can make you give us the book? Make it easy on yourself and your family. Give us the book and all the copies you've made. Keep your mouth shut and everyone will live happily ever after."

CHAPTER 25
ESCAPE

Pam's mind raced at warp speed. She must decide what to do. In a flash it came to her. She stood and walked to the desk facing Harris. He looked up at her without speaking.

"I'm not going to leave here alive!" Pam shouted at the top of her voice. "You've told me too much to let out of this in one piece. You didn't hesitate to kill my parents. You won't hesitate with me."

"I told you all we want is that damned book. That and the bullet you dug out of the Burris' wall. That's all. Then you can go. Then we won't need you anymore."

Pam continued to scream, "You stupid ass. Do you think I'm that dumb?"

Harris was livid. He stood and shouted back at her. "Will you sit down and shut your mouth, or do we have to shut it for you?"

Pam grabbed the goose-neck lamp with both hands. With all of her strength she swung it at Cobra's face. Her aim was perfect. The bulb exploded in his face with a flash of light. Cobra Harris fell to the floor writhing and screaming in pain. Both hands grasping his burned and bleeding face.

In the dark, a hand grabbed Pam's shoulder. "You stupid bitch, what in the hell do you think you're doing?"

Pam spun around, the lamp plug pulled loose. Again with both hands she swung. This time her target was Dutch. She connected with his head.

"Hey, dammit stop that, have you gone crazy?"

She swung again and again, each time hearing the metallic 'thunk' of the lamp landing on Dutch. She followed as he backed away. The crash of a lamp and overturned table indicated he had tripped and fallen to the floor.

Pam threw the lamp aside and ran toward a narrow sliver of light. The drapes by the French door. The door opened. She raced through the rose garden, slid over the gate, and reached the side of her SUV. Parked next to her was a BMW. She got in her car. The keys were where she had left them. "Start baby, start." The engine fired. In her rearview mirror she saw lights go on in the library. At the gate she faced traffic from both directions. The few seconds she waited seemed an eternity. With a break in the flow of traffic she pulled onto Kennedy. In her mirror she saw the BMW's taillights light. "Oh my God here they come!"

Traffic on Kennedy Creek Road was light. Pam moved around other cars making good time to Highway Seven. Without having to stop, she pulled onto the highway headed toward Arlington. By the time she reached the Dulles toll way overpass, traffic had picked up. At Tyson Corner she saw a car behind her, weaving in and out of traffic, slowly gaining on her. As she approached Interstate Sixty-six, it appeared there were few cars on the highway. Without slowing speed, she drove up the ramp and onto the freeway. Pam pushed her speedometer to over eighty.

There were headlights behind her. Were any of those cars Dutch's Beemer? She was now in Arlington. At Lee Highway she left the interstate, again ignoring the posted exit ramp speed limit.

Pam spoke out loud. "I've lost them. My best bet is to go up to Glebe Road, take that over to three ninety-five and straight down to Springfield. There I know where to go. Oh God, what a night."

Her first bad break came at the intersection of Lee and Glebe. A stalled car caused her to wait through two lights. A few minutes down Glebe she saw it again. A car behind her, moving back and forth through traffic, gaining on her. She drove faster, but the other car matched her speed, and then some. It still gained on her. When she went under highway sixty-six again, where it snakes through south Arlington, it was only two cars back. The highway was commercial on both sides. It would remain like this for miles. Traffic was steady in both directions. Pam knew she had to chance it. Her SUV could not outrun Dutch's BMW. She waited as she watched oncoming traffic. There was a break ahead. She slowed, staying in the left lane, her pursuer was in the right lane, one car behind her.

Pam took a deep breath. "Now!" With both hands she pulled the steering wheel to the left. Her vehicle slid in a tight U-turn, heading in the opposite direction. The front wheel drive pulled her vehicle along, but her rear tires skidded dangerously on the pavement. An acrid odor of burning rubber filled her car. Miraculously, the car stopped fishtailing in the middle of traffic.

Pam drove three blocks past a stoplight, switched off her headlights and, without touching her brakes, turned on a side street. She went a few blocks to a stop sign where she pulled to the curb. This should be a through street. Now she must wait. Maybe nobody will turn this way. She jumped. "Oh damn!" A car had pulled into the side street and rapidly approached her. With lights still off, she moved to the corner and turned right. Once more she pushed her gas pedal to the floor. In three blocks she pulled the wheel hard to the right heading back toward the traffic light on Glebe. It was green. A block away the light turned yellow. In her rear view mirror she saw the other car turn the corner behind her. By the time she reached Glebe, the light was red. Pam closed her eyes and went through the light. She never heard the horns, screeching tires or epitaphs hurled at her. She opened her eyes and sped down the street in darkness. The other car had not made it through the intersection.

After a few blocks she turned left, went a block, and turned left again, then back right. She continued her zigzag pattern until she was a block south of Glebe. Lights still turned out. Any other time a cop would already have stopped her. What should she do? Pam feared if she headed for Springfield, they would be waiting somewhere. If she tried to find the cops, what could she tell them. Nothing that would make any sense. Cobra might have already called them. They may be looking for her now, thinking she was some kind of a spy or terrorist. She couldn't keep pace with her thoughts.

Ahead she saw parking lot lights. The back entrance to a supermarket. She pulled in. To her right appeared to be employee parking. She backed into an empty space, between a pick-up and a van. The parking lot entrance and some of the back street were visible. It would be hard for anyone to see her.

She knew they were out there looking for her. How many does he have now? They've certainly had time to get reinforcements. Pam's advantage was they didn't know where to look. She knew she couldn't go home. Pam jumped as a car pulled into the parking lot. It was a family. She turned on her parking lights. The dash lit up. Ten twenty-eight. She sat in darkness. Every vehicle that came in or went by made her start. Ten forty four. Pam pressed her forehead against the steering wheel and moaned. "I can't handle this anymore. My nerves are shot. Dammit, I did the very best I could. There's just nothing left inside."

With a deep sigh, Pam took her cell phone from the consol. She pressed auto dial, then the number three. She listened to the musical notes, then the ringing. On the third ring a female voice answered.

"Petersen residence."

"Gabby, I've got to talk to Brad!"

A hushed voice spoke, "Honey, its Pam."

"This is Brad."

"Brad. You've got to bring me in!"

CHAPTER 26
SAFEHOUSE

The phone was silent for a few seconds.

"What happened?"

"They were going to kill me."

"Who?"

"Mark Harris and Dutch."

"You clean?"

"I think so. I used the moves you told me and I believe they worked, at least for now. I thought I'd lost them before, but they keep turning up again."

"Where are you?"

"In a supermarket parking lot, somewhere on Glebe."

"You're not sure where?"

"No. I've wandered back and forth for what seems like forever."

"Okay. Are you west of highway three ninety-five?"

"Yes."

"Have you passed Columbia Pike?"

"No. What is this, twenty questions?"

"Not quite. If you miss one of these, you lose more than prize money. Listen close now. Stay off Glebe. Come onto

Columbia Pike. Turn north and go five blocks past Glebe. On your left will be a motel, Commonwealth Inn. It's L-shaped. Are you with me?"

"Sure. But what's Commonwealth Inn? Why there?"

"It's a safe house. It's not in the greatest area of town, but I've got to get you under wraps. Did you meet someone named Elliot at Cobra's place?"

"I saw him. He gave me the creeps."

"For good reason. I only found out about an hour ago he works for Harris now. We think he may have killed a dozen or so people, some of them he tortured to death. These are guys you don't want to fool with."

"Well, that's just great news to hear."

"You need to know what's going on. When you get to the motel, park next to the van out front. Your SUV will be pretty well hidden from the street. Got it so far?"

"Yes, go on."

"Take your car keys in your hand when you go in. If anything's not just exactly like I'm going to tell you, or if something doesn't seem quite right, go back out to your car and leave. Tell them you need to get your purse or something. Then call me again as soon as you can."

"Why do you think Cobra would know where I'm going? I didn't know until now."

"It's not Cobra. We use this place a lot. Any number of groups would like to blow the cover on one of our safe houses. You ready?"

"Yes."

"Go in like I said. If nobody's at the front desk, ring the bell. When you see somebody, tell them you need a room. They'll tell you they have no vacancies. You say you have a reservation. They'll ask your name. Tell them George Washington."

"You mean like George Washington slept here?"

Brad chuckled. "You're way too smart. They'll want to

know your confirmation number. Say it's Petersen, four seven two eight. Can you remember that?"

"Yes. Do I need to know what it means?"

"No. Let's hurry up. I've got to get you out of that parking lot before they drive by and find you. The person will say okay, or some such, and ask you which room. Tell them the one with the best electronics set up. Are you ready to go?"

"Do I have a choice?"

"No you don't. I'll see you there later. Good luck."

Pam switched off her cell phone, took a deep breath, and pulled out of the parking lot. She did not like the idea of going back on the street. What if she stopped at a traffic light and they pulled up next to her. A mile down the road she came to Columbia Pike. Pam had to wait for a break in traffic, and crossed Glebe again without having to stop for a red light. After a few blocks she saw the Commonwealth Inn on her left. There was no way to cross through traffic there. Pam drove two more blocks to a light, made a U-turn, and at the motel pulled in beside a van. There were only five other cars at the motel. "Forty-seven twenty-eight, forty-seven twenty-eight," Pam repeated as she walked into the small lobby.

A man stood behind the counter reading a magazine. When Pam walked in, he looked up, smiled, and laid his magazine on the counter. *Sports Illustrated - Swimsuit Issue.* He appeared thirty something, short black hair, square jaw, stocky, and decidedly clean cut. He looked like he might be an FBI agent, a cop, or a Marine. Maybe parts of all of them.

Pam returned his smile. "I'd like a room please."

The man checked Pam from her red toe nails to her slightly mussed hair. "I'm sorry ma'am, but we're all filled up tonight."

For some reason the man made her feel safe. She

returned his gaze. *Well at least I'd rather him look at me instead of his stupid magazine. I'll bet he doesn't think I'm a mousy brunette.*

She pushed a lock of hair from her forehead. "I have a reservation."

"Name please?"

Pam swallowed hard. "George Washington."

On the verge of being jovial he asked, "And I guess you have a confirmation number?"

For the first time in hours Pam felt almost relaxed. "Yes I do, forty-seven twenty-eight."

Pam smiled at the man again. But only for a second. His expression had changed completely. From the almost boyish smile, his face turned grim. His jaws clamped shut as he thought for a few seconds.

"I'm sorry ma'am, I missed what you said."

Her almost relaxed attitude of a few moments ago had vanished. She was suddenly tired, very tired, and functioning on raw nerves. She should be Ricky's Cub Scout den mother, not hiding from a bunch of killers.

"I'm sorry. This has been one hell of a night." She took a very deep breath, closed her eyes, and recited, "It's Petersen four seven two eight."

He laughed out loud. "All right. You scared the shit out of me ma'am. Excuse my French. We sit here night after night, nothing happens, then somebody good looking walks in and we can get a little off guard. When you blew that, you kind'a took me back. You need a room?"

Pam resisted pointing out she had said that when she walked in. In spite of her combined exhaustion and fear, she laughed. "Yes, I need the one that has the best electronics set up."

"That's number two. This way."

The man opened a door leading into the motel and motioned Pam to follow him. Two doors down on their right he stopped. A brass number two was attached to the wall. He unlocked the door, pushed it open, and reached in for the light switch. Pam had no intention of entering the room first. He must have read her mind.

"I haven't been in this one for a while, let me check it out." He walked in. Pam stepped inside and looked around. It looked more like an efficiency apartment than a motel. To her left was a closet, small apartment kitchen unit, and a bathroom. The man had gone into the bath. Facing her were drapes, a love seat, an easy chair, and a small desk. To her right, a bed, night stand, and chest of drawers. On the other wall was a TV and a panel containing plugs, jacks, switches, and dials. That must be the electronics. In the center of the room stood a table and four side chairs. The furniture was plain, functional, and sturdy looking.

"The bathroom has everything you need." He turned on the TV. It was a baseball game. "Yankees, wanna watch 'em for a while?"

"No thanks."

He walked over to the small refrigerator. "Soft drinks, ice, couple of beers, what have you. Do you wanna pot of coffee? I've got some made."

"No thanks."

"I'm going back out front. Lock the door and throw the dead bolts. Don't open the door unless you can recognize whoever's out there through the peephole. If I'm coming back, I'll call first. If you need me, dial the operator, it rings at the front desk. I'm going to let Petersen know you're home. Okay?"

"Sure."

"By the way, my name's Cal."

After Cal left, Pam looked at the door. Sheet steel. She knocked on the walls. Concrete block. She pulled the drapes back, more sheet steel. The room was a dungeon, but a very safe dungeon. Pam could feel her last strength ebbing. "I'm not ashamed, and I want my mother. I'm scared. I never thought it would end up like this."

She fell back in the easy chair. Sleep came in seconds. Not a deep restful sleep but rather the fitful slumber that comes with mental exhaustion. First Dutch, then Cobra, and finally Elliot waved meat cleavers and chased her down the hall of her high school. Then the bell rang, class was over, everyone disappeared. Pam sat upright.

"What the hell's that?" she said aloud. "Oh it's the phone." She walked over and picked up the receiver. "Yes?"

"This is Cal. I talked to Petersen, he said it's gonna be about an hour. You all right?"

"Yes, I'm fine."

"I'll call you when he gets here."

This time her sleep was less traumatic. When the phone rang again, she calmly answered it. "Yes."

"They're here. I'm bringing 'em back."

She waited at the door and looked through the peephole when they knocked. In the hall she saw Brad, next to him a woman, behind her a tall balding man with a pleasant expression, she couldn't quite see who stood behind Brad, in the rear was Cal.

"Hey Pam, it's Brad, open up."

She undid both dead bolts and opened the door.

"Well you don't look too much the worse for wear."

"Maybe not on the outside, but the inside is about shot to hell."

"Don't blame you. Pam, this is Maggie Tadlock, she's from my shop and has been working on the case. This is Rod Kinney, one of the FBI's best electronics experts. And this long drink of water is Bill Williams with the IRS."

They each acknowledged Pam in turn.

"The IRS?"

"Hey don't sell us short Pam. Ness didn't get Capone, it

was the good old IRS." He laughed.

"Unfortunately it may come down to all that we have is tax evasion." Brad said. "But since this is criminal fraud, we could still burn them really bad."

"Ten years maybe," Williams added.

Brad spoke with authority, "It's late. Let's get to work. Maggie can you help Pam off with her hardware?"

"Sure. Come on." The women went in the bathroom and closed the door. The electronics expert placed his cases on the table, opened them, and began working. Bill sat in a wooden chair and watched. Pam and Maggie came out of the bathroom.

"This is some set-up," Maggie said. "I've never seen anything like it before. The mike's the size of a dime and hooks on the front of an underwire bra where the wire acts as an antenna. This tiny wire goes down your front and the recorder tapes inside your panties. The recorder's smaller than a book of matches."

"It's still in the test phase. Hasn't been issued to the field yet. I had one at home experimenting with it. We didn't have time for me to go to the office and get something else."

The woman grinned. "Did you help her get rigged up? I doubt anybody could get this on alone."

Pam blushed.

"No, Gabby helped her."

"I don't think that's quite by the book is it boss?"

Brad's next comment made Pam spin around with her mouth open in surprise.

"After six years as an undercover agent, Gabby has done and seen just about all of it. Hell, she was a better field agent than me."

CHAPTER 27
THE UNLIKELY AGENT

Pam regained her composure. The expression on her face was incredulous. "I didn't know Gabby had been an undercover agent. I knew she worked for the FBI, but not as an agent. Why didn't she ever tell me that?"

"A lot of what she worked on is still sealed. She knows it's better not to talk about anything, then you don't have to worry about what you're saying. Anyway, for the last month or so, don't you realize that you've been an undercover agent too?"

Rod looked at the tiny recorder. "This is a beauty. I guess you didn't think to bring any literature on it did you?"

"There isn't any. Just how to attach it to someone, turn it on and off. What's the problem?"

"It's so small and sensitive, the least overload of current will fry its insides. I've got to use very low power, and slowly step it up until we get a usable dump. I'm going to load it to my hard drive so if I accidentally overload, we won't lose everything." He adjusted dials on his equipment. "Simultaneously I'm going to burn an ultra-resolution disk.

Using that we can pinpoint the times we need to listen to, filter out all background noise, and amplify anything that needs analysis."

"Such as?" Brad's interest in his new toy grew.

"I can filter out Pam's heartbeat, her breathing, her stomach noises, and anything else in the room that would cause background static. Something like the ticking of a grandfather clock."

Pam blushed again. "I don't make stomach noises."

"Everyone does. It's your food being digested. For example, we can identify the make and model of a refrigerator in another room just by the sound of its motor. Now, all of you be quiet. This takes my complete concentration."

"About how long?"

"Maybe thirty to forty-five minutes."

Brad looked at Pam. "How long were you in the house with Cobra and Dutch?"

"About two hours."

"What all did they tell you?"

"Everything. From Vietnam in 1971 through yesterday."

"What about the book?"

"Everything, except who the other people in the book are." Pam hesitated. "They also told me that Dutch killed my parents."

"I'm sorry, Pam."

"Right now I'm just glad to find out the truth. Do you think we can get him?"

"Ask me again when I know more what there is to work with. Now we will definitely have to listen to the whole tape. It's after midnight now, by the time Rod gets set up and we listen to the tape a few times we're good for all night. Maggie, would you call Cal, have him bring us coffee and get some sandwiches from that all-night deli down the road? That all right with everybody?"

When no one protested, Maggie went to the phone.

Brad turned to Pam again. "You're stuck here for the night. Do you need to contact anyone? Anybody expecting a call tonight?"

"No. I talked to Ricky early and Rick's on a late night dinner cruise. I probably should check the answering machine just in case. As soon as Maggie gets off the phone I'll do that. Then that's everything."

"No. Where's your cell phone?"

"I left it in my purse locked up in the car. Why?"

"By now Cobra knows you've given him the slip. He knows you won't go to your house, even though he probably has somebody waiting for you, just in case. What he does expect is that sooner or later you will check your messages. I'm certain by now they have your phone bugged. When you call, they will trace the call and be on you like a bunch of flies on a piece of watermelon."

"That's poetic, but I thought you had to physically get to the phone to bug it and my security system's on. Anyway doesn't it take several minutes to trace a call?"

"You forget, we're dealing with the CIA. They will go to a junction box where your line runs and tap it. Tracing the number on the other end's almost instantaneous."

"They'll get the number of my cell phone, won't they?"

"Sure, but they won't know where it is? Let's go out and get your phone. I'd guess you could use some fresh air by now."

Pam agreed. "I need my purse, too."

When Maggie finished, Brad talked to Cal. "Wilson and I are coming out for a while. All clear?"

Brad hung up and walked to the door. While Pam opened the dead bolts, Brad took an automatic pistol from under his jacket and released the safety.

"That looks just like Gabby's pistol."

"No, mine's a nine millimeter, hers is a .380."

"Oh, I should have seen that immediately."

"You must feel better. You're being a smart ass."

"I can't help it. I grew up in a home where humor was a standard way of life."

"Don't ever change. There's not near enough humor in the world. Maggie, could you lock up after us please?"

***

When Brad and Pam returned, the coffee and sandwiches had arrived. "How's it coming, Rod?"

"So far, so good I guess. Just slow 'cause I've never seen this thing before."

They picked up a sandwich, poured some coffee and sat on the love seat.

"Brad, when this ended you were going to tell me where all the pieces fit. I think it's over now."

"You're about right. I'll get the book from Malone in the morning. Shouldn't take long to unravel it using what we'll know by then. We can't use your tape as evidence, but it should tell us where to look for the other parts. So, for all practical purposes, you're out of this."

They ate their food in silence.

"Ready for the rest?"

With her mouth full of ham on rye, Pam nodded.

"From the look on Rod's face he may be getting close." Brad took a drink of black coffee. "Can you handle me talking directly about your father?"

"A month ago, no. Today, yes." She picked up another half sandwich."

"When your father called the FBI, he got one of the people who works for me, David Durant. David came to me with the story. A retired Army Colonel had information about money laundering going on in high levels of the government. We did a quick background check on your dad. Certainly not a crackpot. He was coming in on Thursday. Then he called David and changed it to Friday. Then he called again and changed to Monday. Your father began losing credibility. The police didn't find them until Saturday, so it hit the papers on Sunday. David called me at home. I met him downtown. Sure enough it was the same Bill Anders who wanted to talk to us.

"First thing Monday morning we opened an investigation. On Tuesday word came down to pull back, it wasn't a Federal case. I went to my boss with what we had and convinced him to talk to the Director. He got back to me, no dice. Word had come from someone way up in Government to knock it off. In the Bureau you either play by the rules, or you leave."

"Why did you ever talk to me then?"

"When the Breaker story came out, I tried the waters again and got shot down again. That smelled really bad to me. People normally don't tell the Bureau to pound sand. I could take the first time that it wasn't a Federal crime, but this time I knew something had to happen. Then Gabby told me who you were. At first I suspected you might be involved, but Gabby convinced me to the contrary.

"When you came up with that hair-brained scheme to sting Breaker, I thought maybe we had something. Since I had to keep hands off the Anders case, I had to contract with you undercover to find Breaker's sources. Not the murderers, but the story on the money. If we could find out something on that, maybe it might direct us to who killed your parents. Everything fell in place on its own. We got you with Malone to let him lead you after the murderers, if that could be done. Then you stumbled on the book. You already know the rest of it."

"Given the restrictions you had, how did you ever get me under contract?"

"We have more than forty offices worldwide, and almost all of them hire local nationals for a variety of tasks. Everything from clerical work to overt and covert operations. Nobody blinks an eye. Is there any reason why we shouldn't do the same thing here in the United States?"

"I guess not, but I don't think you answered my question."

Brad smiled at his wife's best friend. "That's all the answer you'll get. And believe me, that's all you need to know. By the way, I do think you're also entitled to an explanation of why I let you go to Harris's place without cover."

"I think so too."

"After what you learned from Breaker and Morris, I did some checking into your father's seventy-one activity in Vietnam and later in Bangkok. While with AID, your dad had a dotted line relationship to the CIA and a guy named Mark Harris. Harris was also in Vietnam in seventy-one. Station Chief for a CIA operation. Back then he had no link to your dad, but it certainly was a coincidence. We figured Harris had some information, maybe money laundering, he felt he should share with you. See, at that time we still believed Khan or his people were connected with the murders. We thought Harris might have the link to someone high up in government."

"You mean because of the way the door got slammed shut on your investigation attempts?"

"Yeah, pretty much so. Now we know it wasn't Khan at all; Harris and Vortmann had committed the perfect crime when they killed your folks."

"Okay, how?"

"When the police investigated the murders, they must have talked to Dutch about the phone calls. He would have said something like, 'Hell I've known Bill Anders for over forty years, I talk to him all of the time.' Then he could tell them about Harris, that your dad used to work for him. That would have explained the asterisk phone calls. No one ever looked any further."

"So without me you never would have solved the murders?"

"That's right, for the last month you were our undercover agent that blew the case wide open. Maybe the world's most unlikely agent, but an agent none the less."

"I was scared to death the whole time. Yes, you're right, I'm really a wife and a mother. I must have been the most unlikely agent of all time."

"Eureka!" shouted Rod.

"I believe he's ready to run the disc now." Brad and Pam walked to the table.

Lights blinked, the audio started with a loud crunching noise. Rod jerked his head at the machine.

"What in hell's that? I don't think I've ever heard anything like that before."

"I turned the recorder on when I walked to Cobra's house. That's me walking on his gravel driveway."

Rod shook his head and looked at Pam. "I can tell this will be some night."

Bill moved to the foot of the bed and the other four took the wooden chairs. They listened in silence. Pam was commended for finding and unlocking the French door leading to the rose garden and her car. Frequently Brad or Maggie had Rod replay portions of Cobra's comments. Rod stopped the disc once to point out that the gurgling sound was the stomach noise he had mentioned earlier. Pam, as usual, blushed.

Toward the end of the recording Pam said, "Rod , could you pause it please. I missed this at the time, but how did Cobra know I had found the bullet?"

"Who all knew about you finding it?" Brad asked.

"Malone's out of town so I couldn't call him. Only Joan

Burris and I knew." Pam put her hand to her mouth. "Oh, then she must have told Dutch!"

"Sounds that way. Let's go on."

When Cobra talked about the killing of her parents, Pam's eyes watered. Everyone remained silent during Pam's belting the two men with the gooseneck lamp until Bill said, "That sounds like a scene from a Woody Allen movie." They all broke up in laughter.

When the chase came on, Pam excused herself to the bathroom. All she wanted to do was forget it ever happened. How on earth had she managed to do that?

Pam walked back into the room to hear Brad. "Rod, you did a great job. Thank you."

"That's what they pay me for. I've got it on hard drive and a master. Tomorrow I'll enhance the hard drive copy. You'll probably have use for the CD."

"Uh-huh. Maggie could you get the CD to clerical support and have them make a paper copy transcript?"

Maggie agreed.

"Bill, what do you think?"

"Not too good, not too bad. That money will look like it came from offshore charitable trusts. To begin with we'll probably have to argue if it's even taxable. Our best approach will be to audit that Trust Company of Dutch's. What we find there should get us into the offshore records. It's most likely Bermuda. If it is, good, they cooperate quite well. From there we'll have to grind it out. Unless one of the twelve cops a plea, it's a long drawn out process."

"How can you just walk in and audit someone? I thought the law had changed?" Pam vaguely remembered when she worked at Justice the talk about curbing IRS excesses.

"Oh no, no, of course not. The trust will be randomly selected." Bill looked at Pam, bobbed his head, and grinned.

"What do you think about bringing Dutch to justice now?"

"Good question Pam. Their world is falling apart. Somebody may turn on him or, given that we now know what to look for, more evidence may be out there. If it is, we'll find it. What I want first is to get a search warrant for Dutch's condo. He's the type who's apt to leave the wrong thing laying around. Frank Malone will have a big part in this, starting with shaking up the Mount Vernon police with that broken clock, the fourth bullet, and Mrs. Burris, who will probably sing like a nightingale."

Pam's eyebrows arched. "Malone's with the FBI?"

"No. We use him in situations where we have to be on the sidelines. Same as we did with you. He'll be perfect for this. He can claim client confidentiality, somewhat like a lawyer, and keep you out of sight."

"What about our safety. You've told me these men are killers."

"We checked your phone every day. It had not been bugged so it's unlikely they know where Rick and Ricky are."

"I mentioned it to Dutch at lunch, but I doubt if he was listening. Anyway he got too drunk to remember anything. Why didn't they bug my phone?"

"Probably didn't see any reason to. You were a nuisance to them, but not a threat, until they knew you had the book and that bullet. We're dealing with some bad actors, but not the Mafia. Except for Cobra and Elliott the rest will turn tail and run. Elliott works for whoever pays him. If Cobra's going down, Elliott's history. Cobra we can keep under surveillance."

Pam looked at her watch. "It's after four in the morning. You're right, it was only yesterday morning I saw Harold Timmons. It seems like years. Brad, I'm running on raw nerves now."

"That's understandable. We'll be gone in a few minutes. There are some clothes, don't know what, in the chest. Tomorrow someone will take you back home. I'll be out your backdoor. Also, I think I'll have an agent camp out over there for a while. Anything else?"

"No I'm just thankful it's all over. Now I want Dutch and the other people responsible for my parents' deaths to be punished. And I'd still love to punch Ned Breaker in the nose. Anyway Brad, thank you and Gabby for seeing me through this. It was rough, but I'm glad I did it."

"Don't thank me for letting you go to Cobra's alone. If I'd had any inkling what was behind this, I would have had a backup waiting outside the wall. You were great. Will you ever tell Rick? We can probably keep your identity undercover, so that's your call."

"Let me sleep on it. For now get your friends out of here before I pass out."

"We'll be on our way in a couple of minutes."

As he turned away, Pam stopped him. "Brad, where will this whole thing end?"

He looked back. "Eventually people like Mark Harris, Dutch Vortmann, and their friends go too far, they take one more step and land over their heads. As I said, their world's finished and so are they. I'll let you know as things develop."

CHAPTER 28
HOME

Pam watched through a front window as the school bus rolled to the end of her street, stopped, turned on its blinkers and slowly disappeared around the corner. It was the third day of school. That summer program had paid off, Ricky already knew many of the kids at his school on the first day. Fortunately he and Adam were in separate classes, they would see too much of each other if they weren't. Ricky, Pam thought, needs more friends, like the redheaded girl down the block, Jana. Pam smiled. Jana had invited Ricky and Adam to her birthday party next week. The boys said that Jana wanted to invite only boys. Her mother made her invite some girls too. *Kids grow up too soon now,* she mused, *Ricky's in the fifth grade, boy does that make me feel old, but just wait 'til he's in high school.*

Pam walked back toward the kitchen where Rick was finishing breakfast. It had been fifteen days since that night in the Commonwealth Inn. To Pam it seemed like years. She had not seen Brad since then, but had talked to Gabby almost every day. Gabby said things were moving along. They brought what they had to a seated Federal Grand Jury.

According to Gabby that was going okay, but she couldn't talk about it. They were also trying to get a search warrant for Dutch's condo. Pam wondered if it had been issued.

"Hi baby, have you read *The Review* yet?"

"No, I've been busy feeding my men and getting Ricky off to school. Why'd you ask?"

"This is from Breaker's column. It's not long, only one paragraph, I'll read it to you. But first get another cup of coffee and sit down."

Pam did as directed.

"Ready?"

"I'm ready."

Rick cleared his throat and read. "On the fifth of July my column hinted at the possibility that the late Bill Anders, and his wife Betty, had been murdered due to underworld connections. Recently I have learned the information provided me was deliberately erroneous, and that documents given me proven false. This was not done to harm the reputation of two fine people. No, it was aimed directly at me. A cheap attempt to undermine the years I have spent developing unquestioned integrity and honesty. I offer my sincere apologies for any harm that has come to the Anders' family due to the work of those who sought to discredit me."

"What kind of BS is that? And what documents? Even when he's sorry, he's still a jerk."

"Wait that's not all of it. On the bottom of page one. Get this. I quote, 'The Management of *The Washington Review* regrets to inform our readers that Ned Breaker is no longer associated with this newspaper, but has resigned to pursue other opportunities. His hard-hitting column, 'Exposé', will be sorely missed. We wish him the best of luck.' How about that?"

"Well I'll be damned. What do you think really happened? You have any ideas?"

"I would guess that he just screwed up one time too many and *The Review* canned him. You feel vindicated, I would think."

"You're damn right. Before you go to work let's talk about Japan. Isn't this great?" She picked up one of the several travel pamphlets lying on the table.

"I'll say, and it came right out of the blue. Old man Ito was so excited about the merger that he invited the whole bunch that worked on it to Japan for a week at his expense. Isn't that wild?" Rick made no attempt to conceal his excitement, but then, neither did his wife.

The back door banged. "Hi guys, anybody home?" It was Gabby.

They greeted her in unison.

"Do you have a few minutes?"

"Of course we do."

"Coffee?"

"Sure Gabby. Grab a cup and sit down. What's on your mind?"

Gabby picked up a pamphlet. "First, tell about the trip. Was this a surprise or what?"

Rick refilled his cup and sat back down. "Wednesday night the Japanese company took everyone on a dinner cruise to celebrate. After dinner their president, Charley Ito, announced his company was taking their new venture partners on a week long trip to Japan at Ito's expense. Charley's English is only fair. It wasn't until Goldman and I were in a taxi going back to the hotel that he told me the Japanese also invited one of our firm's partners. I figured it would be him. Then he asked me to have dinner with him Thursday. He took us to a place in Fisherman's Wharf where they charge you to say good evening." Rick laughed at his own humor.

"Richard, please get to the point. Our plane leaves tomorrow afternoon."

"Old miss subtle there. To make a short story even shorter, he said he and his wife Ruth had been to Japan, and she's having problems with her knees so the trip would be a real hassle for her. Since I'm going to be named partner in a few months anyway, Pam and I should go on the trip."

"What did you do then?"

"Since you're not allowed to kiss a senior partner in public, I thanked him all to hell and back. Now what's this rumor I heard yesterday that a certain Brad Petersen's going to be named Deputy Director of the FBI? Seems he's the hero of the hour."

Pam clapped her hands in excitement. "Really, Gabby that's wonderful!"

"Except it's not true. They offered the position to Brad, but he said no thank you. That position's just like being Director. It's ninety percent political. If you get along with the President, then it's great. If you get sideways with him, then you're out of work. Brad said President Allen would be all right to work with, but if that guy Goff goes in next, well that could be a problem. He and Brad have already had differences."

"Oh, Gabby I'm sorry."

"Don't be. Instead, Brad's going to be promoted to a GS-15 job. There's only three in the bureau. The guy that has it now is going to become Deputy. Directors and Deputies come and go, but GS-15's are civil service. They stay. On a day-to-day basis, they run the bureau. That brings me to why I'm here. You sure you have time?" She looked at Rick.

"Sure, I'm just cleaning up loose ends today. I can be a little late getting in."

Pam threw her hands in the air. "Boy, he already sounds like a partner."

Rick gave his wife a mock dirty look. "Shush, go on Gabby. Just ignore the magpie."

"See what you won't get in Japan for that remark." Pam stuck her tongue out at her husband.

"If you two can stop playing for a minute I do have information. Brad planned coming over, but he had to go in early for a meeting with the Director. They're going to court today to seal the files that contain the identity of the undercover agent that broke the money laundering operation here in DC."

"I've heard talk of that. So it's true?" Rick inquired.

"Yes it is. The Federal Grand Jury will bill nine people this morning with three more expected this afternoon, some technicalities need to be worked out. Obviously the people being charged had an inkling something was up. That man Timmons your dad worked for at the bank, you remember him?"

"Uh-huh."

"He got drunk and tried to commit suicide, botched it, and ended up shooting off a little toe."

"You are kidding?"

"No. I think he turned states evidence after that. Now get this. Have you ever meet a man named Niles Carter? He's with State."

"Yeah, I met him that night at the Goff's. A cocky, arrogant little snot."

"That's the guy. He got to the Canadian border with a fake passport, phony mustache, and dyed hair. The border patrol got suspicious because he looked so stupid and searched his car. In the trunk, where the spare tire should be, they found over two hundred thousand in cash and another forged passport."

Rick had listened with limited interest. He realized that if Pam were at the Petersen's bragging on something Rick had done, Brad would be polite and listen. At any rate Rick wasn't ready to go to the office yet. "What's the deal with the other three? Why haven't they been billed?"

"I can't say a lot, but Brad would tell you this much, they're in the Government."

"Isn't that guy Mark Harris with the CIA? That's Government."

"I know, but the other three are elected officials."

Rick's interest was aroused now. "I'll be damned, the Grand Jury's going to indict a congressman or some such today."

"No. Brad said he believes the Grand Jury will have the officials testify in person on their behalf before any action's taken."

Pam frowned as she spoke, "What if they claim their rights under the Fifth Amendment and refuse to testify?"

Rick and Gabby looked at each other. "It's your story Gabby, go ahead and finish."

"This isn't a Congressional hearing. If you claim the fifth to a Federal Grand Jury, you're automatically billed. All they have to do is determine reasonable cause. If you say you might incriminate yourself by talking, that's reasonable cause."

"And if they lie?"

"With all of the evidence the jury has, that would sound a lot like perjury. If they tell the truth somebody will probably go after a RICO conviction."

Pam pursed her lips. "That sounds to me like a prime case of lose, lose, lose."

"These people must be complete idiots," Rick said.

"You would think so. There's more. Mark Harris and Dutch Vortmann denied having a fight. They claim they were assaulted at Harris' house but they won't say who did it, or why."

"How do you know all of this?"

"They were taken to the emergency room. Harris got hit in the face with a lamp. The bulb exploded, burning his face, and the glass cut him up pretty good. Then somebody hit Dutch in the head with the lamp. Took fifteen stitches to close the gashes in his forehead. Now for the climax." Gabby paused for dramatic effect. "Are you two ready for this?"

"Yes Gabby go on. You're getting as bad as Rick."

Gabby ignored the comment. "They got a warrant to search Dutch's condo. In one of the bedrooms, in a box he hadn't unpacked since he moved in, they found a 22-caliber automatic pistol, still loaded. The police did a ballistic test on bullets fired from Dutch's pistol. They matched the ones that killed your parents. It would appear that what you heard that night about Dutch killing them might very well prove true."

"Gabby, you have no idea what a load this is off my mind. It's like a new world has dawned. I wish I knew what to say to you."

"Don't worry. I remember the first time I met you at the spouses' luncheon. The way you looked then compared to who you are now tells me everything. I love both of you so much. You're going to bring Ricky over after school today?"

"That's the plan. You sure you don't mind keeping him for a whole week?"

"Heavens no. The two of them are easier than Adam by himself. 'Mommy I'm bored. Mommy come do this, Mommy come do that.' No, no problem. Anyway after this money laundering thing's put to bed, Brad and I want some time together. Guess who we will ask to look after Adam?"

"Just let us know."

"I've got to run. I know you two have a million things yet to do." Gabby hugged Pam, kissed her cheek, and disappeared out the door.

"Your friend's something else. She always like this?"

"Always. She's the most dynamic, versatile, and interesting woman I have ever met. My mother would have loved her."

He would never mention it, but Rick had noticed the ease with which Pam could now handle the loss of her parents. For the first time in more than two months, he knew she would be her old self once more.

"Explain to me again how you got into this mess. I understand what Gabby said, at least most of it, but I'm still not completely clear where and how you got into it."

"I told you this once, but it was probably mixed up a little. The week you went to San Francisco, Dutch invited us to a reception at Mark Harris' house."

Pam paused. She and Gabby had developed her story and Pam must tell it exactly the same each time she was questioned, and she hoped this would be the last time she would have to lie to Rick.

"Go on honey."

"Sorry, I was thinking about the trip. Anyway, he called Wednesday to see if we were still coming. I thought meeting some people who might be of value to your practice was a good idea. In this city you can't know too many people. Dutch picked me up. When we got to Harris' place, I lost him. While looking around I walked up to the study, I think. Anyway, through the door I could hear two men arguing. One was Dutch. He called the other one Cobra. They went on about money they were laundering through Dutch's Trust Company. Daddy had mentioned the Trust Company to me and how Dutch spent so much time on it for no apparent reason, but not the money laundering, of course. Then Cobra says, 'If you hadn't wasted the Anders like that we wouldn't be in this mess now.' I almost fainted; I couldn't believe what I heard."

"I can certainly understand that. It's almost unbelievable. What happened next?"

"I was in a daze. Somehow I got to a phone and called a taxi. Then I told someone that worked for Harris to tell

Dutch I got sick and went home. When I got here, I didn't know what to do. You were on that dinner cruise somewhere out in the Pacific Ocean, so I called Gabby and Brad. Seems Brad had an inkling of some of this. You know the rest. Is it clear now?"

"I think so. Pam I'm so glad that you didn't keep fooling with this after you saw what's-his-name Morris. These people are bad news. No telling what might have happened to you."

"I'm tired of this. Let's talk about fun things."

"Like what?"

Pam slid onto Rick's lap. "Like why you called me a magpie. I thought magpies were ugly, had warts, and talked all the time."

Rick slid his hand into Pam's blouse. "No, not at all. Magpie's the muse who used her sexual prowess to drive men insane with animal lust."

"You're right, I am a magpie, in fact, a damn good magpie." She put her arms around Rick's neck and kissed him. Several times.

"Hand me that cell phone will you?"

She handed Rick the phone.

He pushed buttons to melodic beeping. "Hello Matty? . This is Rick. I've got some things to take care of here so I'll be later than I planned."

Pam put her mouth over Rick's ear.

"Uh . . . Uh . . . after lunch, I'll be in after lunch. Bye."

"Watch it counselor. This magpie's gonna get ya."

CHAPTER 29
SUBPOENAS

A black sedan pulled to the curb. Three men exited the vehicle and stood on the sidewalk. The older one looked at his watch. "We told them three thirty. It's close." He looked at one of his companions, a dark-haired man. "You have the papers?"

The man patted the front of his jacket.

The third man, whose ruddy face and reddish blond crew cut made him look almost adolescent, asked, "Tell me again why we're doing it here?"

"He said he thought it would be better here with all three of them rather than some official place."

"How did he get mixed up in this anyway?"

"Petersen said it started when he was a Senator and Chairman of the Ways and Means Committee. When he moved up, they picked up the new Chairman as a member."

"Why Ways and Means?"

"They make the tax laws. It's time, let's go."

The older man walked up a few steps to the front door. The other two men looked at each other, adjusted their jackets, and followed. He pushed the doorbell and a maid in a crisp black and white uniform opened the door.

"Yes sir. May I help you?"

The first man held up a leather card case. "I'm Agent David Durant with the Federal Bureau of Investigation. This is Federal Marshall Lopez and Federal Marshall Kelly." The other men identified themselves as they were introduced.

"Yes sir, they're expecting you. This way please."

The maid led them down a hallway to a heavy wooden door. She rapped on the door. From inside came a slow southern drawl. "What is it Alena?"

"The government men are here to see you senator."

"Oh yes, please show them in."

Alena pushed the door open and the men entered the room. It was a library, or a study, as one might name it. Bookcases filled with leather bound books, paintings in expensive frames and Persian carpets, all intended more to impress than for function. The room was dominated by a massive mahogany desk surrounded by several leather side chairs. Two men sat in the chairs. One a slender balding man with glasses, continued sitting, merely glaring at the new arrivals. The other, fleshy, ruddy, with a shock of silver hair, rose and faced the agents.

"Senator Prentiss Puckett the Third, of Kentucky at your service, gentlemen. This gentleman, is my colleague, Congressman Eb Goodman of Georgia."

Agent Durant repeated his introductions, then turned to Lopez and nodded. Lopez took two sets of folded paper from his coat pocket, selected one, and faced the senator. "Sir you are hereby ordered to testify before a seated Federal Grand Jury at the place indicated hereon, on the date and time also so indicated. Failure to comply with this subpoena may be considered contempt of court subject to a fine and possible imprisonment. Do you have any questions?" He handed a piece of paper to Puckett. "Would you sign this please?"

"You people will not go away, so I may just as well sign it and get this over with." With a sigh he took a gold pen from the desk, scribbled his name and handed the paper back to Lopez.

Lopez handed the senator another piece of paper which the senator shoved into a jacket pocket.

Goodman's pinched face turned crimson and he shouted, "I'm not going to sign any of your damn pieces of paper so don't bother asking. This is not Nazi Germany, you Gestapo thugs can't break the door down and strong arm a United States congressman like I'm some petty drug dealer."

Puckett glared at Goodman. "Dammit, Ebenezzer you knew as well as any of us this could not go on forever. The day would come when the piper must be paid. That, my dear friend, is today. For once in your miserable life do something like a man. Sign the paper and don't embarrass us. We'll have our day in court."

"Give me the damn thing and give me a pen."

Lopez selected another set of papers. He handed a sheet to Goodman. "Sir, you are hereby - -"

"Shut up. I heard what you told whiskey breath. I don't need to hear it again." He scratched some lines on the paper and threw it and the golden pen on the desk. "Is that all? Am I free to leave or do you have some other shit to do?"

Durant replied. "No sir, you are free to leave if you wish."

Goodman opened the door and looked back over his shoulder.

"I want you Nazis to know that I will have your ass and your jobs over this. Remember that." He slammed the door.

"After twenty years of winning elections, some people can't be good losers. Please forgive his somewhat rude behavior."

"No problem senator. It's after three thirty, do you know where he is?"

"Telling his wife. He put that off to the last possible minute. Knowing her as I do, I would imagine he's catching the very devil right now. Not even my wife can spend money with the flair she has. No, his wife's not going to take this well."

Silence filled the room. Puckett sat down and studied his well-shined shoes. "Oh well, it was one hell of a ride while it lasted."

Kelly looked at book titles, Lopez and Durant stood and waited. A door at the end of the library opened. A tall, distinguished man entered the room.

Senator Prentiss Puckett stood and faced the new arrival. "Gentlemen, may I present the vice-president of the United States, the Honorable Trevor Goff."

THE END

Pam Wilson is back again and, once more, up to her neck in trouble.

Turn the page for a preview of Pam Wilson as *The Unlikely Sleuth*

THE
UNLIKELY
SLEUTH

A Pam Wilson
Mystery Novel

by
William Walker

CHAPTER 1
CLAUDIA

Pam Wilson poured herself a second cup of coffee, sat at the kitchen table facing her husband, and reached for a section of the morning's *Washington Review*. Nothing in this calm, routine morning prepared her for what she saw next.

"Oh my God, Rick!"

"Huh?"

"You remember Claudia Lloyd?"

"Daniel Lloyd's wife?"

"Yes. She was murdered last night!"

Rick dropped the sports section on the table. "Are you serious? Who in hell would do a thing like that?"

Pam scanned down the article. "The police don't know. Daniel was out with clients and when he got home late he found her. Oh Rick! They shot her in the face with a shotgun." Pam turned ashen and her hands shook as she handed the paper to her husband. "You finish it. I can't read any more."

"They have a picture of her. She was good looking wasn't she?"

Pam blinked back tears. "Yes, at least she had been. Guess at one time she was drop dead gorgeous, but when I knew her she looked hard, worn, like somebody who's had a tough life. Sorry, I'm babbling. Finish the article."

She realized Rick was trying to divert her from remembering the morning she found her parents brutally murdered. Shot to death in the house they had shared for twenty years.

"You got most of it. Daniel came home and found her on the kitchen floor. She must have walked out of her bedroom and caught some prowlers. No suspects. Most likely crack heads according to the police, but they always say that these days." Rick looked up from the paper. "You okay, baby?" He handed her a paper napkin. "At one time you knew Claudia pretty well didn't you?"

"Sort of. We worked with Ruth Goldman on your firm's Christmas party last year. Guess we were together a dozen times or so. Most of 'em at Claudia's house, the house where they killed her." Pam broke into tears and placed the napkin over her eyes.

Rick walked to his wife, put his arm around her, and cuddled her head to his chest. He took several deep breaths. "Are you all right now? I mean, this reminds you of your folks doesn't it?"

"Yes." Pam wiped her eyes, pulled away from Rick and sat upright in her chair. "I finally came to grips with that. Daddy had discovered those men were laundering all that drug money. When they found out he knew and that he wouldn't take a bribe, they killed him and mom to keep him quiet.

"This is different. For about four months Claudia and I saw a lot of each other. Ruth always left our meetings first. After she was gone, we would go out on Claudia's flagstone veranda and have a glass of wine. Since Ruth was allergic to smoke, Claudia could finally have a cigarette."

Rick stood looking at his wife. As much as he loved her, he also knew as his firm's newest junior partner he was expected to be in early, and stay late. He poured himself a fresh cup of coffee. "You want another one?" he asked.

"No thanks. Anyway, I did sort of get to know her. We talked girl talk and all, but she never opened up. Seemed to keep a wall between the real Claudia and the world. But since the party, and that was what, nine months ago, I haven't even seen her. But last night she's alone in her own home, hears a noise and goes to check it out and . . . oh God, nobody should have to die like that."

"I know. It's terrible. But unfortunately life isn't fair, shit happens." He finished his coffee and stood up. "I've got to get moving. You will be able to handle all of this, won't you?"

"Of course, you know I will. Don't you think we should do something?"

"Yeah. At this moment I can't grasp what happened. Daniel's a partner, one of over a hundred. I barely know him well enough to say hello, but still . . . I don't know. I'll have Matty find out what the firm's doing and call you, okay?"

"Good. Give me a hug and a kiss before you leave."

He tousled her hair. "That's a given."

CHAPTER 2
THE ALLEY

It's after six, let's call it a day."

"Sounds good to me." Pam pushed a lock of hair from her forehead and looked at Lindsey Sims, owner of The Book Place.

Lindsey was tall and willowy. Brown hair reached to her shoulders. Her oval face was highlighted by two very brown eyes, photogenic cheek bones, and a sensual mouth that mirrored every mood. Her high school yearbook labeled her vivacious. A very apt description.

The Book Place reflected Lindsey. Shelves of brightly covered books and an aroma of a potpourri made the first impression. A far corner contained a kindergarten size table and chairs, the children's corner. Several soft leather chairs urged patrons to sit and browse.

Pam worked part time in Lindsey's bookstore. The women had become friends in collage so when Pam moved two miles away, she was happy to help out. Having mad money that didn't come out of the household budget was nice. She liked getting out with people, loved books, and most of all, thoroughly enjoyed Lindsey's sometimes zany company.

Lindsey was exuberant. "Pam, thank you a zillion for staying late. Can you believe one little article in the *Review* could bring in this many people? I can't believe it! Before you go can you take the trash out back? I've got to total today's sales."

"No problem." Pam picked up two plastic bags of trash and walked through the shop's rear door into an alley which ran the length of the strip shopping center housing The Book Place. Dirty boxes, discarded newspapers, and empty bottles of cheap whiskey shoved into little brown paper bags cluttered the alley. The stench belonged to the back streets of all big cities. To her right was a dumpster, now being assaulted by Jason Sowell. His gondola cart was heaped with plastic garbage bags and filled the better part of the passageway. Pam edged around the cart, tossed her bags into the trash, and turned to face Jason. "I can't believe Wee Ship It generates that much garbage."

"If I ever got around to emptying it out more than once a week it wouldn't be so bad." Jason Sowell was young and slender, in his early twenties, with a shock of sun bleached hair, blue eyes, and a boyish crush on Pam. "Dana said you and Lindsey had a stream of customers all day." Pam caught Jason's glance drifting down to her sleek legs.

"Yeah, that article in the *Review* paid off. People were in and out all day. We were almost as busy as you guys are every day." While Pam would never encourage Jason's interest, she was, none the less, flattered.

"Ain't no biggie. More dudes ship stuff than read stuff." Jason stopped feeding bags to the dumpster and now occupied himself with Pam.

"Have you decided what to do about school this fall?" She frequently wondered if her ten-year-old son, Ricky, would be like Jason when he grew up. Attractive, intelligent, articulate, but not well focused on tomorrow.

Jason moved around his cart and leaned against the dumpster facing Pam. "I've been thinking about Old Dominion, but I'd really hate to leave - - "

A car horn shattered the relative silence of the alley. Pam and Jason turned to see a large black sedan whose progress was blocked by Jason's gondola cart.

"Yeah man, just a minute." Jason hurried around the cart and grabbed its handle. His first tug turned the cart enough to jam a wheel under the edge of the dumpster.

The black car, a Lincoln with a noticeably dented right rear fender, revved its engine and honked again.

Jason continued trying to maneuver his cart free.

"Look-a you shit head, move dat damn thing or I'm gonna run you skinny ass down."

The voice had an accent vaguely familiar to Pam.

"You hear me now! Move it kid!" More honking.

Pam flushed and started toward the car. Her first instinct was to protect Jason. From who or what, she had no idea. An electric window on the right rear side of the car moved slowly down. A female arm slid through the opening. The disembodied hand flipped a lighted cigarette butt toward the dumpster. With erratic aim, the smouldering orb headed toward Pam, who squealed and jumped to her right.

"Hey, watch it!"

Before her, in the back seat of the car, sat a blonde haired woman. The woman's ice blue eyes locked into Pam's face for several seconds. Pam stared back in disbelief as the woman looked away. The sedan's window closed, and a black Lincoln sped past the dumpster.

Pam watched as the car, its license plate obscured by dirt and road tar, moved down the alley. A block away, at a dead end, it slowed, turned right, and disappeared.

Jason had gone back to his trash bags. He looked up as Pam, still staring at the now empty alley, walked past.

"Mrs. Wilson, Pam, you okay? That car didn't clip you when it went by did it?" He moved toward her as she passed the cart.

"No. No I'm fine." Pam entered The Book Place's rear door.

Lindsey spun around in her chair facing Pam."You won't believe it, but this is the best Thursday I've had since I opened." With a start she jumped to her feet. "Oh my God, what's wrong? You saw one of those big nasty black rats didn't you? They're disgusting, but unless you get 'em in a corner where they can't run, they won't bite you or anything."

Pam dropped into the worn leather chair in Lindsey's cramped office. Her pupils were dilated and her breath came in short gasps. Her head slowly shook left to right.

"Pam, you need some brandy? I've got a bottle in my desk. What in the hell happened to you? Oh no, it wasn't one of those filthy bums or street people was it? They scare the hell out of me. No, security's suppose to keep them away now. But if you saw one of 'em we've got to call the cops."

Another head shake.

"Hey, was Jason out there? He didn't get smart did he? He tried to hit on me once and I had to straighten him out. I've seen the way he looks at you sometimes." Lindsey stood and hovered over her friend.

"Lindsey - - "

"Yes?"

Pam looked up. "Lindsey, you remember Claudia Lloyd? The woman I told you about a month or so ago?"

"Sure. Your friend . . . your friend who was . . . murdered?" Lindsey's voice trailed off.

"Yes, dammit. Lindsay listen to me, Claudia Lloyd isn't dead. I just saw her in the alley."

PRE-PUBLICATION ORDER FORM

The Unlikely Sleuth is scheduled for
publication in only six months.

To reserve your autographed copy contact the author
William Walker at bwalker72@aol.com
or the publisher

Outskirts Press
www.outskirtspress.com

Please provide an e-mail address, a snail mail address, or a
telephone number, so we'll know how to contact
you when it's hot off the press.

The Unlikely Sleuth pre-publication price is only
$12.95, plus shipping costs.

Thank you for your interest and support.

Printed in the United States
140548LV00002B/74/A